The Valley

Estampas del Valle

Rolando Hinojosa

The Valley

Estampas del Valle

Rolando Hinojosa

Arte Público Press
Houston, Texas

The Valley is made possible through a grant from the City of Houston through the Houston Arts Alliance.

Recovering the past, creating the future

Arte Público Press
University of Houston
4902 Gulf Fwy, Bldg 19, Rm 100
Houston, Texas 77204-2004

"The Border Door": site specific performance/installation/intervention. Media: gold painted wooden door, hung and framed, keys. Chicano artist Richard A. Lou placed a workable freestanding gold painted door with 134 detachable keys on May 28, 1988 on the Mexico/U.S.A. border, 1/4 mile east of the Tijuana International Airport. After installation of The Border Door, Lou returned to the house of his youth in la Colonia Roma and distributed over 250 keys, inviting people he encountered to use The Border Door, as he walked to La Casa de Los Pobres in la Colonia Altamira. Both neighborhoods are in Tijuana, BCN. "The Border Door" photo credit: James Elliott.

Cover design by Mora Desıgn

Hinojosa, Rolando
    The Valley = Estampas del Valle / by Rolando Hinojosa.
        p.   cm.
    In English and Spanish.
    Includes bibliographical references.
        ISBN 978-1-55885-787-2 (alk. paper)
        1. Mexican Americans—Fiction. 2. Rio Grande Valley (Colo.-Mexico and Tex.)—Fiction. I. Hinojosa, Rolando. Estampas del valle.
    II. Title. III. Title: Estampas del valle.
    PQ7079.2.H5E7913 2014
    863'.64—dc23
                                                            2013038549
                                                                  CIP

♾ The paper used in this publication meets the requirements of the American National Standard for Information Sciences—Permanence of Paper for Printed Library Materials, ANSI Z39.48-1984.

First edition published by Quinto Sol Publications, Berkeley, CA, 1973
Second edition published by Justa Publications, Berkeley, CA, 1977

14 15 16 17 18 19 20   10 9 8 7 6 5 4 3 2 1

Contents

To Patti, Clarissa and Karen Louise, again

PREFACE

Some forty years ago as a young graduate student, I marveled at the literary world represented in Rolando Hinojosa's *Estampas del Valle* that seemed to have sprung from nowhere. Here were characters, a language and a setting that had never before been the material of literary arts. Never in my wildest dreams did I think that one day I would become the publisher of *Estampas* and of all the subsequent works written by Rolando Hinojosa. I fondly remember that at a 1973 conference on Tomás Rivera and Chicano literature, Hinojosa said that he would be delighted if someday I would write about his works. Many years passed before I could take him up on that invitation. But more importantly, since the early 1980s, Arte Público Press had inherited the mantle of Quinto Sol and published the works of Rolando Hinojosa. Now it is my pleasure to add a few lines to the volumes that have been written in many languages about Rolando Hinojosa's creative world.

What you hold in your hands, dear reader, is one of three foundational works of Chicano fiction, having won the Quinto Sol Award that forever designated Rolando Hinojosa's *Estampas del Valle* (1973), along with Tomás Rivera's *. . . y no se lo tragó la tierra* (1971) and Rudolfo Anaya's *Bless Me, Ultima* (1972), as *the* models for the nascent literary movement that would inspire and guide hundreds of Mexican-American and other Latino narrators for at least the next forty years.

Estampas del Valle and *The Valley*, Hinojosa's re-creation in English of this novel, present a mosaic of the picturesque character types, folk customs and speech of the bilingual community in the small towns in the Lower Rio Grande Valley of Texas. While his sketches and insights are at times reminiscent of the local color *crónicas* published in 1920s Spanish-language newspapers, his experimentation with numerous narrative forms in his various novels that follow *Estampas*, ranging from reporting to epistolary to detective fiction, make Hinojosa's art one of the most sophisticated contributions to Latino literature. *The Valley / Estampas del Valle*, along with the first novels by Tomás Rivera and Rodolfo Anaya, constitute what the Quinto Sol editors hoped would be the basis for a Chicano literary canon, a bulwark for the creation of a Chicano cultural nationalism.

Regardless of the canonicity or not of what were back then marginal, minority group texts at Quinto Sol, they opened creative pathways and were emulated by literally thousands of writers in an effort to provide a language and literary corpus for what had been cast as the "sleeping giant" of Mexican-American and Latino people in the United States. Thus for more than forty years, Hinojosa's writing has served as a model and inspiration for Latino writers of diverse backgrounds. At first, what was noteworthy to scholars was Hinojosa's characters who, despite or because of their apparent isolation from a larger world, were stubborn and unashamed in their affirmation of place, tradition, dialect and worldview. Hinojosa's work even pointed to an apparent Golden Age, a time of cultural origins prior to the coming of the Anglo, when language was pure, traditions were established and a sense of identity and place were well formed. But *The Valley / Estampas* was just the beginning phase of a continuing novel, the Klail City Death Trip (KCDT), articulated through a series of books with different titles and structured in diverse genres that have become a broad epic of the history and cultural evolution of the Mexican Americans and Anglo Americans on Texas' border with Mexico. All of the books in the continuing and ongoing series, with some twenty installations at times published in separate Spanish and English editions (not translations), are centered in the fictitious Belken County and focus on the lives of two characters and a narrator—Rafe Buenrostro, Jehú Malacara and P. Galindo—all of whom may be partial alter egos of Hinojosa himself. What is especially intriguing about Hinojosa's Klail City Death Trip Series is his experimentation not only with various forms of narration—

derived from Spanish, Mexican, English and American literary histories—but also with English-Spanish bilingualism. While there are many Latino writers of historical or generational fiction, Hinojosa is unique not only in developing a multibook and multi-genre trajectory but in articulating his fiction in separate re-writings in English and Spanish of the original texts. Hinojosa's series is not a historical novel in the common understanding of such, in which a narrative is constructed in a remote time period; KCDT evokes and recalls the foundational period of Valley culture and updates it in an irrevocable path toward extinction of the original cultural base, at least extinction of the "old ways" on a path toward a new, hybrid culture in this chronicling of Mexican and Anglo-American culture clash and then blending across the generations. It is the linguistic and ethno-cultural diversity represented in Hinojosa's texts that can only be understood, on the one hand as a synthesis and on the other as a breech between Anglo and Mexican pretensions of nationhood, an interstitial area that speaks and acts for itself and is a cradle of creativity and affirmation beyond national assignations.

The Valley / Estampas del Valle is nothing more than the first chapter of what Hinojosa's narrators would call *El cronicón de Belken* or *El cronicón del Valle*, that is, an ongoing, open-ended epic. Hinojosa's art is not just a simple chronicling of the ebb and flow of two cultures in contact, of farm and ranch and town real estate, financial and legal interests, of families and personalities, their conflicts, marriage lines and separations. Hinojosa's has been a highly literary experiment in which he not only gives artistic form to a life heretofore never represented adequately in literature and art, but his experiment also has involved, nay demanded, seeing how far he can adapt and mold the literary tools he inherited to capture that life at the crossroads of two cultures and two nations. His experimentation has led him to explore and recapitulate the complete history of literary genres, from oral lore and epic to *nueva narrativa lationamericana*, from both the Spanish-language and English-language traditions, from his tipping his hat to *El Cid* and the *Quijote* to Ambrose Bierce, Faulkner and other American writers.

The Valley / Estampas in its apparently simple depiction of endearing characters, regional dialect, subtle humor and irony, has many deeper layers for the reader to explore: anti-clericalism, cultural integrity and sense of place, multiple and fragmented perspectives on what is socially constructed as truth. . . . But most of all, *The Valley / Estampas* is an entertaining and intriguing read that needs no philosophical or literary analysis to be enjoyed.

Nicolás Kanellos, Ph.D.
Publisher

Born between two worlds, one dead and one as yet unborn.

—Matthew Arnold

ON THE STARTING BLOCKS

The etchings, sketches, engravings, et al that follow resemble Mencho Saldaña's hair: the damn thing's disheveled oily, and, as one would expect, matted beyond redemption and relief.

A WORD TO THE WISE (GUY)

What follows, more likely as not, is a figment of someone's imagination; the reader is asked to keep this disclaimer in mind.

For his part, the compiler stakes no claim of responsibility; he owns and holds the copyright but little else.

An Olio

One daguerreotype plus photographs

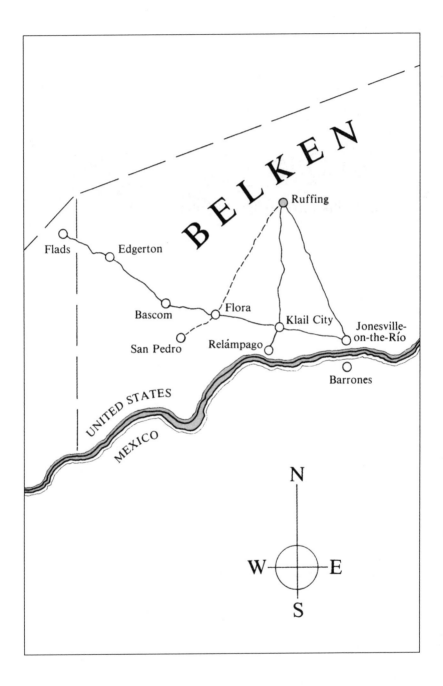

BRAULIO TAPIA

Squat, what the Germans call *diecke* and thus heavy of chest and shoulders, Roque Malacara carries his hat in his hand; this last shouldn't fool the reader, however, since R.M.'s step is firm and resolute.

I'm standing on the doorway on the east porch of a hot Thursday afternoon, and he says: My coming here alone isn't a matter of disrespect, sir, it's just that I've no money for sponsors.

He then asks me for my daughter Tere's hand; I nod and point to the living room. Hat held in a firm hand, he follows with the same and sure unwavering step.

He then reminds me that I gave him permission to call on Tere: it's been over a year and a half, sir. Again I nod and this time we shake hands.

Turning my head slightly to the right, I catch a glimpse, or think I do, of my late father-in-law, Don Braulio Tapia: long side-burns and matching black mustache á la Kaiser; Don Braulio raises his hand to shake mine as he did years ago when I first came here to this house to ask for Matilde's hand.

By that time, with Doña Sóstenes' death, he'd been a widower as I now am and have been since Matti's death years ago. Don Braulio nods, takes my hand and bids me enter.

Who did Don Braulio see when he walked up these steps to ask for his wife's hand?

TERE MALACARA NÉE VILCHES NORIEGA

I'm bushed, beat and dead to the world; know what I mean? I'm a dollar short and three days behind, and I can't even blame it on staying up, which I don't, anyway. It's this life, that's all. It's hard.

I know there are other women worse off . . . still . . . well, take the barmaids, now. Why, they're pawed at by anyone with the price of a glass of beer. Or, and maybe worse, the housemaids. It's known that neither danger nor the devil blink an eye, and the housemaids had better not, either: I mean, there's the Mister and the Mister's son, and (I know what I'm talking about) it's best to keep an eye on the Mrs. herself, you bet.

Yeah, I know that the servant girls and the barmaids are worse off, but what's that to me? I'm both dog and bone tired, and that's a mortal fact.

Now, if I were educated I'd be able to say this much better, wouldn't I? Finer, maybe, but the trouble is, I'm just plain tired.

ROQUE MALACARA

Tere's my wife, and I know she's tired. S'got every right to be so. We only have the boy now; Tere and I have now seen to the burial of my father-in-law and our three girls.

My father-in-law was a good man; a good man in the best sense of the word *good,* as Machado once pointed out. He loved to fish the sly Río Grande gray-cat; his favorite companion was his little namesake, *our* Jehú, since each had the patience to bait and hook the trickster feeding in the tules.

Now, if there is such a thing as reincarnation, I'd swear, and I would, too, I'd swear that my son and my late father-in-law are one and the same person.

LYING TO WITH SAILS SET

The age of seven may be a mite early to meet Death head on, but that's when I first met her; it happened of an early evening when I finally arrived home from school by way of the estuary and the canal, stopping for a long swim in each. The women of the neighborhood were standing in the middle of the street waiting for me: Don't go home, now, Jehú; we'll call you. In the meantime, you go on over to Gelasio Chapa's barbershop. You wait there, now. And I did; I knew what was up, knew it right off, and I cried the better part of the night until they came for me; I was then fed and tucked but not in our house.

I'd forgotten all about Pa, and when I did ask, I was told: Well, he's been drinking for the last two days, see. He's over at Cano's place, but it'd be better if you let him be for now. And I did that, too.

We, Pa and I, buried Mama not too far from San Pedro, and then Pa and I'd go over there once a month until he, too, one day— and I mean, one-two-three, just like that—, when one day, as I said, he died as he was telling me a joke; a joke which now, some twenty-five years and two wars later, I've not been able to recall for the life of me.

I was about nine when he died, and it was by mere chance that a knockabout carny troupe pulled into Relámpago on that same day.

It was a small affair, the carny was; it included a fair to middling Big Top, and the main attractions were the high wire and the trapeze acts. The wire'd be strung out the length of the eighty-foot tent and a man (made up to look Japanese or as if drunk or something) or a girl sometimes dressed up in a one-piece bathing suit would show up and each one behind the other would then wend their way from one end of the tent to the other and back again. The wire was strong and tight enough, all right, but it wasn't too high off the ground.

Now, right behind a cotton curtain, a five-man ensemble played whatever had been agreed upon before the start of the show, and then the curtain would drop, the instruments would be set aside and the musicians, dressed and painted up as clowns, would come bounding out to meet the public. They wouldn't come out empty-handed, either. Each one carried a basket jammed with boxes of caramel candy; the boxes were not always hand-filled to the top, but they were attractive: when flattened out, the customer had himself a Mexican flag as a souvenir.

At other times, other men, or perhaps the same ones, depending on the size of the troupe on any given trip, the men, as I was saying, would stand in the middle of the main and only ring and localize their jokes, that is, they'd joke about actual people or characters from Relámpago or from any of the other neighboring Valley towns. They'd carry on so that the Relampagans, a dour lot, would smile in recognition, nudge each other and, finally, burst out laughing—but doing this was hard work 'cause Relampagans are hard to please.

The thing is that once we buried Pa, and I was brought back to town, I was left alone there, in the park, and the people went off to work or, as we say: they went off to live, *a vivir.*

Well, I walked around a bit; I thought about school somewhat, but then decided to call on my Aunt Chedes on the chance my cousins would be there. (Aunt Chedes never attended funerals; it was her fear that if she did, then everyone there would die. Everyone, she said, and so she always stayed home, ironing).

When I stepped in the house, I almost bolted out the same door I came in because, truth to tell, her crying made me uneasy, ill at ease. Although I missed Pa very much, and I did, I used to look at him as an older brother; one I never had. The point being that my memories of him must've been quite different from those of Aunt Chedes' and of that I am certain.

After a while she stopped her crying, but, and again as always, she had a case of hiccups. And there she was, breathing in and breathing out, when she stared at me for the longest time; she turned to the wall for a moment as if looking for something and then she looked at me again. Well, I figured she was fixing to faint or something, but she was frightfully absent-minded, too, and then looked past me, and I thought she was planning to go off in one of those trances of hers. I stopped her by walking right to her, and asked: "Where's the kids?"

She recovered, was about to explain this end of it, when she stopped her ironing, placed her middle finger—all of it, to the hilt—inside her mouth. She then placed the iron on the trivet and, finger in mouth, she turned, opened the walnut ice box and proceeded to fill a tall glass of water.

The house was quiet, and she hadn't said a word in about five minutes. Placing the glass on the ironing board, she dipped that middle finger in the cold water, made the sign of the cross in the air and then on my forehead: Drink this, she said, drink this whole glass of water, Jehú. All of it, now, and don't stop till you do. While you're doing that, I'm going to say an Our Father backwards for today's the day you're to meet your new Pa.

I looked at her, but she wouldn't start until I started to drink. Standing there, mouth agape, I didn't know what to do, but—just in case—'cause you never can tell, I took the glass and began to drink as she half-hummed, half-sung out: Amen, evil from us deliver and . . .

ABOUT THOSE RELATIVES OF MINE

Aunt Chedes and her husband, Juan Briones, between them, came up with three uneven chips; the first one was Cousin Bias.

Bias was baptized Bias Briones—so far, so good—but by the time he hit three he was called Hoarsey, there being some growth or impediment in his larynx, and so now—right now—a lot of people who remember him can't tell you his right name. And, in re the last name, well, you can just forget that 'cause it's Hoarsey-this and Hoarsey-that, and that over there; God's truth it is when it's claimed that nicknames are powerful friends or enemies; I mean, they'll sweep names and characters away, if one isn't careful. There's more: nicknames sometimes miss the mark. Completely. This may be due to the mortal fact that there's a bit of everything in God's Little Acre.

Look at this: take Antero de León as a living example. Antero's called Kid Fast, and one can't find a slower Christian than Antero in the whole of the North American continent. Dumb ain't the word, as the saying goes, and about the only fast property in Antero is his color: it's green; and you know the kind I mean, it's the green that grows on copper and that's Antero all over.

Anyway, Hoarsey got himself a job as a truck loader and, later on, as a truck driver. And, once he got that chauffeur's license, why, he stepped back, took stock of the Valley and said: Well, folks, it's been good here, but the next time Old Hoarsey farts, it'll only be heard by people living in Ohio, 'cause that's where I'm headed . . . See you.

My other two cousins were Eduviges, whom we called Edu (no need to point out how *that* came about), and who, later on, in school, was Vicky, that being the closest to Viges; the third cousin, Santos, was called Pepe, but that's harder to explain, and I won't even think of getting into that piece of business.

Kindergarten, however, soon took care of the Santos-Pepe hullabaloo: he couldn't have been there over three hours when he went to the bathroom, and, as long as he stayed there—again, so far, so good—he was still Santos or Pepe. It was the coming out. Old S-P walked into that classroom, and the overhead fluorescents reflected, and thus betrayed, a vague glint of a light liquid working its way down from thigh to knee, to shin, to ankle bone. Wait; there's more: not only was he wearing short pants, but these were pure, one hundred percent cotton khaki, and everybody knows how *that* shows.

Yeah, it couldn't have been over three hours, top, 'cause by the time noon-lunch and recess came about, the word was going out: No more Santos and no more Pepe, went the cry. Hoarsey's brother's name is now Mión, Wet Pants. And Wet Pants or Pants it is to this day. As Pants grew up, he went from hellion to hell raiser to stick-up man until he was caught, arrested, indicted, tried, convicted and furnished with a three-year round trip ticket to Sugarland. Once there, he applied himself and this shows what pride, care and nose to-the-grindstone dedication will get you: Pants learned how to make license plates; yeah, he did, and he was good at it, too. He was the best, and the best there, and the best when he left.

License plate making, though, is a highly specialized field, and Pants soon learned there was little demand for his services out on the street: But he was made of sterner stuff; he decided, as he said, to get himself a job even if it meant starving to death.

So, on his first month out, he became a painter's apprentice, and he stayed out of the beer places, too, that being one of the proscriptions set by the parole board. (In the Valley, the parolee stays out of the beer joints two months straight, and he's home free).

At the beginning of the third month, Pants walks into the Aquí me quedo, buys a round for three or four of the regulars when one of these notices the tattoos; Pants was covered with them.

They looked, and he rolled up his shirt sleeves and his pant legs; he then raised his T-shirt and showed those as well, and one in the back where the word *amor* was misspelled *roma*. No one said a word.

Dis-o-ri-en-ted is what people said they were; the man was covered with tattoos from head to t., and they didn't know what to call him now. When asked, he said he didn't care and recommended they vote on it.

It wasn't what you would call a plebiscite, but it sure had the looks of one as people chose sides as to *what* to call him now that the man was a walking-talking spectacle. (A colorful spectacle is what the local paper called him.)

A vote was taken, witnessed and counted. Pants said that if this had taken place in Flora, instead of here, in Klail City, then there would have been a beauty contest (the Flora people being more organized than the Klail City mexicanos), but he let that pass.

The tally was overwhelmingly for Pants as the official name, and it won by a comfortable margin, e.g., the Rincón del Diablo neighborhood, for one, voted Pants unanimously, and you know what *that* means. The losers took it graciously enough, the name Tattoo was retired and Pants went back to being called just that; to this day, as mentioned earlier.

The third cousin, Vicky, took her time in settling down; and, as a consequence, almost didn't. Flighty may be the operative word here, and there's no use her denying she was Aunt Chedes' daughter. It's absolutely true one can't choose one's relatives, but there's a proverb which hits closer to home: when choosing between a full larder and an empty head, in the natural order of things, take the food since it will keep your mind off worry and hunger. Vicky's hunger was something else.

Her leaving the household was no less dramatic: I came up the porch, and she handed me two small bags. Wait here, she says.

There was Aunt Chedes ironing away when Vicky told her she was leaving home to join a carny troupe. Well! Aunt Chedes fainted, was revived, collapsed again, revived again, farted, yelled, screamed and, wouldn't you know it, she caught the hiccups. There she was breathing in and breathing out, when all of a sudden she said, "Water!" But Vicky just stood there and said, "Sit down, Ma; Ma, sit. Listen, Ma."

Which she did. Now, everyone knows no pain or ache on this earth is going to last a hundred years, and the same goes for hiccups, Aunt Chedes being no exception. When her eyes focused again, she remembered something about the tent show, and looking at Vicky right smack, she 1) requested free tickets for the entire family, and that includes you, Jehú; 2) warned Vicky 'not to hang out with bad types.'

Vicky nodded, and, as time went on, she came through with the carny passes. As to Aunt Chedes' second pronunciamento, Vicky followed the same footsteps of the long-gone New World Viceroys: One must always listen to, but not necessarily heed, His Majesty's advice. Unschooled as she was, Vicky somehow intuited this and other sound machiavellian logic and reasoning.

When Juan Briones learned that he and Aunt Chedes would now be living alone again, his reaction was one of exemplary stoicism which garnered additional credit to my uncle and to that fine, old school: the man leaned back and ordered another beer as well as another dozen oysters on the half-shell.

It's said that many are called and fewer chosen and Juan Briones, clearly, belongs to the latter: the happy few; the chosen.

ON THE ROAD: HARD LUCK, HARD TIMES

"Careful, there, and watch how you hold that jack handle, now. Hold it by the handle, Jehú. That's it . . . Hold on, now. Good. There! That ought to do it. Now, reach over carefully and take the crowbar there (pain-in-the-ass rain) and jiggle it . . . like that, yeah . . . go on; yeah, that's it. Aha! Up, down, good. That's it. You got it; keep it steady so's I can ree-mooo-ve this goddam tire! Will you look at that? I knew it . . . Oh, I just knew it had to be the inside tire. Lord, Lord."

"Careful you don't slip on the mud there, Don Víctor."

"I'll be all right, and it ain't the mud, son, it's that fool rain. Watch it, Jehú; on your toes, now, don't lose them tire nuts, hear? Look at this, I'm what you call *wet*."

"So'm I."

"God's truth and no one else's, but what the hell . . . A flat's a flat. You just remember what the Emperor Cuauhtémoc said when put to the torch: 'You think I'm lying here in a bed of roses, do you?'"

"That's the quote, all right, but it was Moctezuma."

"Ah, well, one o' the two. Come on, tire, cooperate, god-damit!"

"It won't, you know, but cussing helps."

"I'll say—gotcha now, you son-of-a-bitch . . . Ha!"

"Don Víctor, I figure we're six-seven miles out of Edgerton."

"Is that a fact? Ummmmm, watch it, Jehú; grab-a-hold o' that jack, son. Careful, now; you wouldn't want it to slip on you. Damn thing'll kill you, Jehú."

"I'm all right . . . Really; you're the one's got to watch it, though."

"Ah, ah, ah, ahhhhhhh! Out, damned spot—Christ and all his nails—There! Got that damned thing—roll that spare on over, now."

"You're going to need some help on that."

"No, it's okay, you just mind the jack, now. There! (Lord God, is that a norther blowing in with the rain?) Watch it, Jehú; on your toes, now. Let's see that crowbar again . . . Hammer? . . . Got it *IN!* . . . Real careful, now. Slow; slowly, now . . . Slowly . . . Good. Jack's coming down . . . we just needtogetourselvesanotherjack s'all there is to it. Eee-sy, does it, now. (Thank you for the help on the tire, Lord, but, between you 'n me, I could've done without that norther blowin' in.)"

"How we doing?"

"We got this thing licked now, Jehú. Careful, boy, don't take your eyes off that jack; damn thing slips and it'll snap your wrist right off."

"Yessir . . . "

"There, Jehú! We *got* it, all I gotta do now is tighten these boogers, and that's it."

"I'm going to check some of the tarp hooks; I noticed one of 'em was coming loose."

"Watch that traffic, Jehú—a lotta damfools on the road tonight."

Don Víctor Peláez was right, all right: the wind blowing in was a cool one; too cool for the Valley this early in October.

On the opposite side of the semi Jehú Malacara was tying down part of the tarp that had come off on that side of the rig. The youngster held two corners of the tarp and brought them together to where the metal holds were on top of each other; once this was done, he stretched them until they were fastened to a hook which both held and anchored the rest of the tarp as well.

The water-soaked high-top tennis shoes were mud-laden as well, and the mud worked its way in and out of the canvas as Jehú walked around the truck checking for other loose ropes. For no reason at all, he remembered he'd left his cap inside the cab; fat lot of good that would've done, he thought. His hair, wet as it was, was now down to his eyes. Eyes which at once were innocent and wise, perhaps not an uncommon combination in the young.

"How's it going, Jehú? Pretty good back there?"

"Yessir."

"Well, let's get in, then, it's high time we were on our way to Edgerton."

"Don Víctor, what's the time?"

"No idea, son. How does ten o'clock sound to you?"

"Sounds about right, I guess."

"Jehú, what do you say to this: instead of going on this very minute, why don't we stop at some roadside place and buy us some Mexican sausage, *chorizo* and some eggs to keep 'em company?"

"With wheat flour tortillas?"

"With wheat flour tortillas."

"And with a Big Red strawberry soda?"

"And with a Big Red strawberry soda."

"Hot Damn! This *is* the life."

The old International semi-coughed, complained and hacked a bit, but it fired up just the same. Don Víctor headed it on the way to Edgerton where Don Víctor's brother would be waiting—and thinking, most probably—that Don Víctor had stopped off some place to have himself a drink or two.

Jehú Malacara rested his head on the window pane looking at the glare which bounced off the glass. He closed his eyes for a moment and dropped off to sleep before he knew it.

ON-THE-JOB TRAINING

"Hey, now, Jehú, you better take-a-close hold on that chain, there; don't give it any slack, hear? Now, you be ready to jump in case it comes loose or something 'cause you could wind up getting your neck broken or lose an eye or somethin'. Got that? Yeah, that's it; that's the way . . . Right . . . Remember now, don't you let it go slack none; get it to move out, but keep it tight . . . it'll start moving on its own in a minute. The weight of it, see? Nudge it a bit. There! Comes off real easy-like, doesn't it? See that post right behind you? Okay, swing that old chain round it; that's the way. Look, I'll do the same on this post here, and then we'll do the rest o' them together, and before you know it, the tent'll be ready to go up. You'll get the hang of it; it won't take someone like you very long."

"Don Víctor, when are Don Camilo and Doña Chucha coming back?"

"Can't be too long . . . we'll get the permit for the parade and the two-week run here like we always do: Camilo always calls on Don Manuel, he's the local cop here, then Camilo tells him how long we plan to be here, puts down a deposit for the permits, gives him half a dozen passes for the show and that's it; nothing to it, really. Hey, you through with that? Good, come on, now, let's go on over to the ticket booth and see how you're coming along with your talk and all; you got that piece memorized yet? It's fairly long, you know."

"You think I ought to use that megaphone there?"

"Let me see that thing . . . Nah, you don't need this. Go on. Take off, Jehú."

"You think so?"

"Well, you can't very well tell what's inside that melon till you plug it."

"That's true, too, I guess . . . Well'p, here goes . . . "

Don Víctor Peláez boosted Jehú Malacara up the platform, and
the youngster mounted a footstool; once up there, he began to clap
with his hands over his head, the way Don Camilo did it at all the
daily performances.

What Jehú was going to say or whoever said whatever was
going to be said, mattered very little since 1) the carny consisted
of one, and only one, tent; and 2) the people were going to show
up anyway; but St. Thomas, I think it was, once said that the force
of habit is what forges tradition and that no right thinking person
will go against *that* without suffering some consequences.

Frankly, now, what Jehú was going to say was nothing new
either, but people don't appreciate your springing surprises on
them or you're going around breaking their old habits for them;
that's something they prefer to do on their own. Jehú Malacara
(with Don Víctor's help) was to realize this as time went on, and
as will be seen in due time.

"Okay, son, fire away . . . "

Jehú nodded, and he began.

"Ladies and gentlemen! Kind sirs and madams! Distinguished
members and lovers of the arts, esteemed ticket-holders and lastly,
children of all ages! Make way, friends! Line up, now, and watch
those elbows—no pushing, hear! And, please! Quiet everybody!
I'm about to start: The Peláez Tent Show, the cleanest and most
moral of all tent shows; the one and the only real, genuine Peláez
Tent Show—the most prestigious, the one you've selected above
all others, is happy, proud, pleased to present an unforgettable performance! A clean, sanitary, fast-moving show for the entire family! Listen to this: A stellar three-and-one-complete half-hour performance! What do you say to *that,* ladies and gentlemen?
Three-and-one-half-hours of fun, happiness, martial music, somer-
saults and a high-wire act, to boot! Yes! Thrill at the Divine Tere
Peláez sitting-a-top a trapeze at over forty feet above the ground—
why, that's twenty meters or more, good people of Klail City! Seeing is believing, yessir! And no pushing, please! There's enough

seats for all. Thrills, yes! and chills; come one, come all, and just don't lag behind, folks, come and see and enjoy and laugh at Don Chema! Don Chon! and Don Ciriaco! Laugh with Doña Lolita and Don Cuco, and, and, and Doña Cuca, yes, she, too, is here and she brought her keen-eyed dog: Black Spot, brought all the way from Mexico's Federal District, that great nation's capital city. Yes! Black Spot, the smartest, the cleverest and best-trained . . . and listen to this: the most *educated* dog in the world and in all of the visible planets of our present universe! What do you say to that! No expense has been spared, NO SIR! Don't you dare miss this performance you knowledgeable, discriminating and highly informed public of Klail City, Texas, the most beautiful and certainly the most important city in the Valley! Come this way, this very moment, right through here, see for yourself, and honor us, the Peláez Tent Show, with your honoring presence, friends! Remember, now, three-and-a-half hours of good, plain, clean, fun—get your tickets here, RIGHT HERE! Tere will not only sell them, she'll also cut them in half for you! Yes, she will! Careful, now, and do watch your step 'cause there's not many tickets left, but we won't start without you . . . And now? What do you hear? Yes! Music! Music from our own selected band, ladies and gentlemen, lovers and sweethearts from Klail City, right this way where you'll be seated in comfortable chairs painted and numbered individually by me, Jehú Malacara. Yes, I, your humble servant with paint and brush did 'em to a turn! Ho! Ho! and don't forget: we have delicious milk candy with milk made from only the wildest and bravest cows! American candy, too, and national delicacies as well and popcorn with *plenty* of homemade butter in tri-colored bags of all sizes plus our solid guarantee that our candy is made fresh *daily:* taffy, licorice, candy canes with anise, caramel and now the newest novelty from the American manufacturing houses: milk shakes in individual cartons with straws attached for your own personal hygienic use! What do you say to *that?* Is there more? Yes! Yes! Yes! and only because this is the Peláez Tent Show, your favorite of favorites, according to the latest polls! Now, ladies and gentlemen, let me direct you . . . "

"Hold it, Jehú, that's enough. Now, this evening, you just get on that little stool there, jump up and down on one leg, do a somersault or two and watch Camilo go through the routine again. You got talent, kid; let's not waste it."

"You like it, eh?"

"Absolutely. Let's go check those posts and chains again; after that, let's see if we can come up with some empty beer bottles for Leocadio's marimba."

The empty bottles would be rinsed, soaped, washed again and then filled with water to some determined levels to give off musical sounds when struck with rubber mallets, like the ones the doctors use. Leocadio Tovar (on the stage: Don Chon) huffed and puffed in the brass section, but when it came to playing the marimba (the mallets were his, and his alone) he had decided long ago that talent would never get in the way of gusto. And, of course, his never did.

BUT SINCE HE DIED

I was going on my third year with the Peláez Show under the patient and paternal guidance of Don Víctor when Death came calling again.

Don Víctor, a tall man, and remarkably thin for a beer drinker (class which, ordinarily, runs to fat) was an upright, honest man who took his liquor, his friendships and his responsibilities straight, which is to say, without benefit of water.

It was because of him that I learned to read and, later on, to love the habit of reading; I started off by reading labels from patent medicine bottles and medicinal herb cartons and, still later on, he provided me with newspapers and magazines of all types and sorts; in short, I read whatever came my way.

Now, if my comings and goings (as Satan almost says: up and down and in the streets of Relámpago) had taught me something, my formal training and education, and what social manners I had come up with, were due, in no small part, to that man.

An early veteran of the *Revolución*, Don Víctor and an old compadre of his from the state of Coahuila (Don Aurelio Alemán) bought and sold horses as a sideline; one of their ventures was with Don Jesús Carranza, a brother of Don Venustiano.

Back there, in the Spring of 1920, Don Víctor, a lieutenant colonel at that time, was stationed in the Papantla, Veracruz, Military District; his stay in the Veracruz and Potosí Huasteca regions was of short duration, and part of my readings came from notes and attempts at a diary which he kept off and on during his stay there. It was through these readings, then, that I learned of Don Víctor's marriage to Lía Samaniego, a daughter and descendant of one of those old Mexican Jewish families. Later on, Don Camilo himself told me that Don Víctor's wife and their son, Saul, and another one as yet unborn, died as a result of the Spanish influenza that (too literally) decimated families, towns and *municipios* during the years 1919, '20, and '21. Something along the lines of the virulent smallpox epidemics that spread among the armies and general populace from 1916 to '17.

What follows is part of Don Víctor's diary; I assume full responsibility for its order (or lack of it) and for a touch-up here and there (commas and the like) although no changes were made in the content, which, after all, is as it should be.

The part here included, by the way, consists of notes taken and set down in the Papantla Military District as well as in Mexico City.

※ ※ ※

Papantla, Ver., 23 May '20

Bad news does travel faster, as they say; word just came in that our fellow Coahuilan, Don Venustiano Carranza, has been shot and killed. No news on who's responsible yet, but we'll know that—and soon—since it happened in this military district. My compadre A., has come up with 27 fresh horses: Mirillas is prob. our best bet as a buyer; my share in this ought to be a healthy one. We'll see.

Papantla, Ver., 24 May '20

Gen. Rodolfo Herrero has been placed in house arrest under heavy guard; orders came right from Gen. Lázaro Cárdenas as Commanding General; the word is that Herrero is the prime suspect in Don Venus' death.

General Manuel Ávila Camacho sent for me early this morning. Orders: as of this very instant, I'm to be in charge, as he said, "of the prisoner Herrero." All I can say is that now with M.A.C. as Chief of the General Staff, the Huasteca Mil. Dist. has two choices: bend or break. It will either tighten up on its soldiering from within or old M.A.C. himself will do it for them; whichever, there's going to be a lot of plain soldiering or they'll just have to start taking their meals in the stockades.

Indian Vela took my civilian clothes out of mothballs; I'm to wear them during off-duty in Mexico City; M.A.C.'s orders will be posted in short order, and I am to be ready to go to M. City when the time comes.

Papantla, Ver., 27 May '20

Nihil novum sub et supra sole, and Obregón's finished his northern swing for the upcoming elections.

Papantla, Ver., 29 May '20

Orders: First leg, Jalapa, where I'm to pick up eight of the 'tried and true': Special guard personnel and reliable, I'm told. Earlier this evening, Pepe Figueroa, a newly assigned civilian attorney on the General Staff took me aside and said that Don Venus was betrayed and thus stabbed in the back literally and figuratively. Well, first off, President Carranza was shot, not stabbed, and *of course* he was betrayed! Does Figueroa think that Herrero and his group asked permission before they shot the old man? For the life of me, I don't understand why anyone in the Gen. Staff could care to listen to anything that Figueroa has to say . . . The horse-trading arrangement is looking better every day; A. says to add another 27 horses to our last count, and that makes it 307. Not bad.

Jalapa, Ver., 2 June '20

Got five of the eight I came for; two are on 20-day leave and one in the local military hospital but hardly for heroism: hemorrhoids due to an overindulgence of cactus pears. As my compadre A. says: Those pears'll get you both ways.

Papantla, Ver., 4 June '20

The five I brought back from Jalapa: Evaristo Garrido H., Relámpago, Texas, E.U.A.; Santos Leal Cantú, Cadereyta

Jiménez, N.L.; Armando Sánchez Villagómez, Jalostotitlán, Jal.; Jesús Balderas, Atenguillo, Jal.; and, Juan de Dios Regüelta, Soliseño, Tamps. Old-line regulars: good, tough and disciplined. These five plus the eleven I picked from here are all I need to take Herrero to Mexico City tomorrow. Early this morning, Indian Vela told me that Herrero was also mixed up with Guajardo in the Zapata assassination a little over a year ago. Probably was.

We're off to M. City tomorrow morning, and Gen. Cárdenas is of the party; he may be in for a promotion. *Note:* special train, special crew; set to leave at 3 a.m.

Mexico City, 10 June '20

Told Felix Cáceres I wouldn't be going out tonight; I can't recall a worse hangover—nor a longer one. It must've been that bourbon whiskey from the U.S.—sweetish and sticks to the palate somehow. But talk about a hangover! From now on I'm sticking to brandy from Coah., or to tequila from Jal.

Putting in for a leave just as soon as this affair with Herrero is over.

Mexico City, 18 June '20

Ten days in this place and nothing to report. Telegram from my compadre A. Good news: money in the bank and waiting for us.

Part of my share is going toward that piece of land near Bella Unión. I'm 33 years of age, been in this war some eight years now, and I've gotten four things out of it: 3 bullet holes below the knee and now this money which my compadre will be sending along.

Knock at the door: Indian Vela just came in with news: Told him to pack. The judge of instruction closed shop today: NOTHING! No *resolution whatsoever.* The judge had thrown up his hands and said there was nothing he could verify or contradict between what either Murguía said or what Herrero contested.

Herrero claims Don Venus committed suicide: four bullet wounds they found. Some suicide.

Mexico City, 23 June '20

   Telegram from Gen. M.A.C.

   15 DAYS LEAVE STOP REPORT PAPANTLA 9 JULY STOP
ENJOY STOP CHIEF GENERAL STAFF MANUEL AVILA
CAMACHO PAPANTLA VERACRUZ

Papantla, Ver., 11 July '20

   Letter from Lía: the priest is pestering her about baptizing Saúl
at the local parish. He's just going to have to wait until I'm home to
stay. I'd no idea that there was still a church standing in Arteaga. It
seems to me that the Dávila brothers blew it up or burned it down
around the time of that so-called barracks revolt in Saltillo back in
'13. I remember seeing one of those bandits in Culiacán: tongue
sticking out right there where One-eyed Melguizo hanged him to a
lamp post. Old One-eyed Marco Antonio Melguizo . . . it was Lucio
Blanco himself who said that Melguizo was one of God's little
unfinished products; a case of being underdone, as it were: he's got
that one eye, he's short three fingers on one hand and two on the
other; his left leg's shorter than the right one, and, when excited, he
stammers, stutters, before he gets going. What Melguizo has, and
no mistake, is a fierce personal loyalty to Lucio Blanco plus a pair
of brass balls & nerves of steel. Will I ever again be or soldier ever
again with those good Northern compadres of mine?

Mexico City, 14 July '20

   Here I am back in the capital city again. Had a ten-minute
briefing yesterday just prior to leaving the Huasteca region; Gen.
Ávila Camacho came by to wish me luck. Am being transferred to
Calles' general staff; Gen. Cárdenas is counting on me not to let
them down. He and M.A.C. wrote letters of recommendation.
That's some Gen. Staff that old Arab's come up with. We'll see.

   No complaints about the accommodations here; it's a family
hotel, clean and cheap.

Mexico City, 16 July '20

Ran into some Northerners; most are from Sonora (as one would expect) the rest are from Nuevo León and Tamaulipas; borderers all. We—the Coahuilans—are more reticent; apart. But: we do share the Northern states' experience, and this helps.

One of them, Cosme Elizondo Carvajal is a first cousin to my compadre A. Three civilian attorneys dined with us last night; youngsters all in their early twenties. By the looks of them, they must've been around twelve or fourteen years old during the Díaz Madero era. And now? Why, they're more revolutionary than the Founders of the Revolution. Oh, well.

Mexico City, 18 July '20

Saw the clothes worn by Madero and Pino Suárez that night in 1913 when they were both shot to death; Grau showed them to me. Grau said the clothes had been found in one of the cellars of the old penitentiary . . . From the evidence, Pino Suárez was shot four times in the back, on the left side; a neat pattern from the holes I saw; point blank, most prob. It started then, with Huerta and that sorry lot of his.

Mexico City, 20 July '20

Lía is unable to join me here; the baby's due sometime in the Spring, and we'll have to wait till then. My father-in-law sent me a Swiss watch with matching gold chain. Showing them off tonight . . .

Indian Vela brought the Orders of the Day for my signature and was surprised to find me up, writing and ready to drive over to the Citadel. First meeting's at 7: it certainly looks as if the Villa affair is not to be resolved anytime soon. At least not peacefully. War? I think so—if it's a shooting war again, I hope it's localized. For the life of me, I can't understand how the Mexican population can stand it or put up with it.

Here's a coincidence for you: brushing my hair and from out of the blue, I thought about the Zapata assassination, & then within half an hour, I received a copy of a telegram from a friend in Monterrey: Guajardo was court-martialed and then shot by a firing squad.

Why a firing squad? They had all the time in the world: they could have just as well hanged him instead.

≫ ≫ ≫

As said, and corroborated by don Camilo as well, his brother lost his family as a consequence of the Spanish influenza. First off, Don Víctor took a three month medical leave and then retired soon after; his military pension was a modest one, and he returned to Arteaga, Coahuila; he remained in that mountain village for five years and never once in all of that time did he go to Saltillo, a mere 15km. away.

When Don Víctor decided to end his self-imposed exile, he emigrated to the United States. As many others before him—and afterward as well, he crossed the river not far from Klail City, in the heart of the Río Grande Valley. As his beneficiary, I received a share of the pension until one month past my twenty-first birthday. Irony: I received the pension checks during my thirty-six month U.S. Army stint.

Age and the aging process never caught up with Don Víctor, according to his brother; and the vitality of the man was there, palpable, even. When I first met him, and when he took me in, as predicted by my Aunt Chedes, he'd been kicking up and down the Valley for some eight-nine years with his brother's troupe.

THREE YEARS WRAPPED IN ONE
TWENTY-FOUR-HOUR DAY

Don Víctor died in the town of Flora; of which more later. After so many peripeteia, it was rheumatism and the chronic liver problems which finally brought the man down. The Habanita Tent Show people and the Furriel Bros. Tent (Vicky's group) paid their respects as well: each company struck the tents, cancelled the shows for that day, and witnessed the burial.

As for me, well, I broke down and cried about as much as when Ma died, and just as heartfelt. The next day, the Peláez Tent Show loaded up and pointed toward Ruffing, but I decided to stay there, in Flora; Death again, orphaned again, and again lying to with sails set.

FLORA

(and why skirt the obvious?) is so called because Rufus T. Klail, guiding light and founder of Klail City, had an only daughter by that name. Some dear hearts say that the town of Flora reflects the same barren aspect of its namesake (who never married): dry, insipid, meaner than the word mean and with what Sheridan called a damned disinheriting countenance.

In Flora, Belken County Texas, many years ago, a train struck and killed some thirty people in a farm truck on their way to work in the fields. One of the survivors, Beto Castañeda, a youngster at the time, hailed from Klail City. Years later he married Marta Cordero, only daughter of the late Albino Cordero. What follows isn't about Beto at all; it concerns the town of Flora itself (one of those wide angle mass portraits) and about what happened there on the occasion of Bruno Cano's funeral.

Make no mistake, the Flora mexicanos do love foofaraws: the larger and the noisier, the better. They celebrate beauty contests for just about every Saint's Day in the calendar; they've got themselves a Mexican Chamber of Commerce, and they're forever holding open air public dances and then they forget to pay the band; also, they organize those seventy-two-hour bingo marathons in the local mission, and if something doesn't need fixing, they'll fix it, and then stand in line to charge you for it.

You know the kind, so why go on?

BRUNO CANO: LOCK, STOCK AND BBL.

"Hold your horses right there, Father. What do you mean you're not about to bury him?"

"Yeah, what about that, Don Pedro—everybody's entitled to at least one burial."

"Not from me, they're not."

"But you're the mission priest, Don Pedro."

"Well, Don Pedro?"

"Listen, you two: you want Cano buried? You bury him. The Church sure won't."

"The Church won't bury him?"

"Yeah, what do you mean that the Church won't bury him?"

(Smiling.) "Listen very carefully: I'm not about to bury him, and the Church certainly won't. Is that clearer now?"

"But you've got to."

"Look! He swore at me, and I'm a priest, but don't forget, I'm also a man—a full-fledged man—of the cloth, true, but a man, for all that."

"Who says any different?"

"Right, Don Pedro—you're a man, and a good one—and a friend to Bruno Cano."

"Just hold it right there, you two. Not only did he swear at me, he then soiled—hear?—soiled my sainted mother's good name. Yes, he did."

"The man had been drinking, Don Pedro."

"That's right, he was overwrought."

"Overwrought? Over—wrought? See here, the man yelled, shrieked, screamed bloody murder at me. And what did I do? I prayed for him."

"He was drunk, Don Pedro. Come on, what do you say?"

"A short service, Don Pedro. Shorter than short."

"No . . . I . . . "

"Go on, Don Pedro."

"Look, we'll all have a drink afterwards. I'm buying."

"Well . . . "

"Come on; we've got him over at Salinas' place; we'll take him to the church, and . . . "

"No! No church. Absolutely not. No, no, no!"

"All right, all right, no church, then. Tell you what, though: from Salinas' place right to the cemetery."

"And what about the hole?"

"Don't worry about it, we'll get it done in time."

"All right, but listen very carefully, you two: from German Salinas' place to the cemetery, and that's it. Now, where's Jehú? I'm going to need him for the response. Remember, now, no church."

"No church."

"Thank you, Don Pedro; I'll send someone to locate Jehú for you."

"No one's to know 'bout this. Got that? No one; fifteen minutes, and down he goes to . . . "

"Thank you, Don Pedro, you're most kind."

"Yeah, don't you worry none and thanks, 'kay?"

The two men left the rectory and headed for the center of town; they neither spoke to nor looked at each other or their fellow townsmen. When they came up to Germán Salinas' cantina, they found that Cano's body was still in the beer locker.

"Good, keep him there for a while longer. We bring good news, as the brother says. We got ourselves a funeral, boys; now, some- one call the Vega brothers and tell them we want their biggest hearse, that's the maroon one with the gray curtains, got that?"

"Now, as for the rest of you, you know what to do: get at that hole, and spread the word."

Don Bruno Cano, a native of Cerralvo, Nuevo Leon, Mexico, and a resident of Flora, Texas, U.S.A., a widower, childless and with no visible or apparent progeny, died (according to the death certificate issued at graveside) of a myocardial infarct that left him like a possum in sull. Now, those who knew Cano au fond said he died of other causes: greed, mostly, and an uncontrollable penchant for skinning his fellowman.

The night Cano died, he and a sometime friend of his named Melitón Burnias had agreed to dig up a plot of ground which belonged to Doña Panchita Zuárez, bone healer, midwife and general gynecological factotum (G.G.F.) and a fare-the-well mender of preowned virgos belonging to some of the neighborhood girls of all ages; virginity is a strict requirement in Flora and thus, we have a simple case of supply and demand.

Now, Auntie Panchita did, in fact, own the plot used for digging, and the Flora types—to a man—said there was gold buried there or near there.

The *relación,* a local usage for treasure, had been there, according to some, since 1) the time of don José Escandón, first explorer and later first colonizer of the Valley, who died with the title given him by the Spanish Crown: el Conde de Cerro Gordo, and whose honored name, etc. etc; 2) since the time of General Santa Anna (Antonio López de, 1795?-1876); Mex. Revolutionist and general; president (1833-1835; 1841-1844; 1846-47; 1853-55). Involved in the War for Texas Indep., the Mexican-American War and under whose leadership Mexico lost the so-called Gadsen Purchase, not to mention the etc. and etc. and the etc.; 3) since yesterday, a conventional term when speaking of the Mexican Revolution (that grand and glorious Crusade for Justice, whose many advantages present-day Mexico now enjoys, etc. etc.) when some greedy-blood-sucking-merchant types who brought gold with them escaping the armies of etc. and etc. And etc., too. Well, the upshot of all this is that one day Bruno Cano and Burnias, a drink-here-a-drink-there, agreed to form an ad hoc partnership as others had in the past to look for the gold that was surely there, had to be there, etc. etc.

The clincher this time was that Melitón Burnias claimed and swore he had recently memorized some infallible prayers for making the earth surrender its buried treasure.

It's difficult to picture more unlikely partners than these two: Cano, plump and running to fat, pink in color, snug with a dollar, and a successful merchant as well as the sole owner of a slaughterhouse called "The Golden Fleece." Summary: one of Flora's most illustrious citizens. Not so Burnias. Burnias was somewhat deaf, on the short side, an indifferent careerist, and

thin and dry / dry / dry

as goat droppings in July.

To add to this, he was worse off than penniless: he was constantly, endlessly, irreversibly poor. He had high hopes, but he also had bad luck, as we say in Belken. For example, when Tila, his eldest girl, ran off with Práxedes Cervera, they were back within the week and, in tandem, the two carried Burnias out to the street and left him there. The man, and this is gospel, shrugged his shoulders, dusted himself off and went to find a place to sleep, which he did: the watermelon patch. That same night, it rained like hail. Burnias, however, was not avaricious—didn't even know the meaning of the word—which may explain why Bruno Cano chose him as a partner in the search for the *relación;* the prayers came as a bonus.

And there they were, at Salinas' place, the two of them drinking away—with Bruno buying—when they were both brought back to earth by the cuckoo clock: eleven o'clock! Hey! We gotta get goin' here! So, out the two partners went to hunt for their picks and shovels and whatnot to try *their* luck at Doña Panchita's lot.

It must've been around three a.m. with Bruno digging and throwing dirt out and Burnias spreading it around the best he could when there came a sound like t-o-n-k! Bruno looked up and then continued to dig some more when t-o-n-k! and he dug some more and that tonk was followed by another and yet another.

"Melitón! Melitón! Didn't you just hear that? I think we're gettin' close!"

"What was that?"

"Close! I said we're gettin' *close here.*"

"A ghost? Near, did you say?"

"What? What did you say? A ghost? Where-a-ghost? Here?"

"There-a-ghost? Oh, *dear!* My God, my God, it's *clear!*"

"A ghost is clear? Is that what you said, goddamit? Melitón? What are you doing? Melitón! Answer me!"

"A ghost? Bruno, I gotta get outta here!"

"A ghost? Did that idiot . . . Jesus! Did he say a *ghost!* Jesus, save me, Lord!"

By this time, Burnias was headed straight for the melon patch and making good time. Cano, for his part, began to scream for help, but Burnias was out of earshot by then: he had cleared two fences clean, had jumped across three fairly wide puddles without trying and he was then chased by most of the neighborhood dogs. One of them strayed off the chase and sniffed near the hole; Cano looked up, saw something and he heard a growl. That did it: Cano not only heard the ghost, he had seen it!

The dog finished his business, turned around and scratched the ground around him, and some fell on Bruno.

"Help! Heeeeeelp! Help me, goddamit! Sorry, Lord. Jesus Christ, get me out of here! Help me, help me out there, somebody!"

It was close to five o'clock now, and here came Don Pedro Zamudio, Flora's one and only mission priest, wending his way to matins when he heard Bruno's screams and cries and curses for help. Don Pedro walked in that direction, peered down the hole and said:

"Who are you? What's going on down there?"

"Is that really you, Don Pedro? This is me, Cano. Help me up, will ya?"

"What are you up to in this part o' town?"

"Look, get me out o' here, and then we'll talk, 'kay?"

"Are you all right? Did you injure yourself when you fell down?"

"What? No, no, I didn't fall down here . . . Come on, help me up."

"All in good time, all in good time. Now, tell me, how was it you wound up down there, and are you sure you're not hurt in some way? I was sure I heard some screa . . . "

(Interruption) "That was me, but I'm okay, really. Now, for God's sake, hurry up and get me the hell . . . sorry."

"And what was it you were about to say, my son?" (Knowingly)

"Nothing, Reverend Father, sir—just get me out o' this hole. Please."

"Well, it's this way: I'd like to, but I don't think I can, you know. I mean, you *are* a little, ah, heavy, ah, a little fat, you know."

"Fat? Faa-aaaaat? Your Mama's the fat one!"

"My whaaaaaaat?"

"Your mother! that's who! That *cow!* Now, get me the hell out o' here! Do it!"

"Speaking of mothers (sweetly), friend Cano, maybe yours can get you 'out o' that hole'!"

"Why, you pug-nosed, pop-eyed, overripe, overbearing, overeating, wine-swilling, son-of-a-bitch! You do your duty as a priest!"

"I will, my son, I will," he purred. With this, Don Pedro knelt at the edge of the hole: First, a rapid sign of the Cross, and skipping the Our Father altogether, Don Pedro started out on the one about . . . "clasp, o' Lord, this sinner to your breast" and then Bruno let go with another firm reminder of Don Pedro's mother. This time, the reminder was as plain as West Texas and the birds stopped at mid trill. For his part, Don Pedro wearing a resigned beatific smile, dug deep and came up with his rosary and, rather unexpectedly, started on the Mass for the Dead; this was just entirely too much for Cano and what started as a low growl exploded into a high-piercing scream directed, variously, at Don Pedro, his innocent mother and any and all relatives dead, living and to come. Cano then gathered another lungful of air at the time that Don Pedro jumped up and extended his arms to form a cross, and, not to be outdone, screamed out: " . . . and *do* take this sinner to your . . . " but Cano did not rejoin; in fact, Cano was still catching his breath or trying to, and by the time Don Pedro finished his latest prayer, he leaned over the hole and asked, "Now, do you see? Prayers *do* bring inner peace, don't they? They've stilled your anger, my son, and tempered both our faiths. Rest easy, the sun will soon be coming up, and so will you."

Bruno was past caring. Somewhere just after one of the mysteries or one of Bruno's motherly recollections, Bruno stopped breathing and thus delivered his uneasy soul to the Lord, the Devil or to Don Pedro's mother. Or to none of the above.

As may be supposed, no less than thirty of us witnessed, so to speak, the sunrise tableau, but we'd all kept a respectful distance while the one chanted and the other ranted.

But, be that as it may, Bruno Cano was buried, and in sacred ground, to boot. To Don Pedro's keen disappointment, the funeral was more than well-attended; and, the damn thing was over seven hours long.

Four orators showed up unannounced but dressed to the teeth: black flower, white hat, gold book, and serious as Hell. Then there were the four choirs (a boys' choir, a girls' choir, one made up of older women, members all of the Perpetual Candle and, the fourth one, an all-male choir from the Sacred Heart Parish from Edgerton; all four choirs were in rigorous white for the occasion, and one would have thought that this was Easter, but no such thing).

The Vega Bros. brought Bruno's body in that wine-colored hearse of theirs; the one with the gray curtains. Besides Don Pedro, there were twelve of us who served as acolytes, and there we were, in white-collared black chasubles heavily starched with backsides to match.

People from all over the Valley got word that something was up in Flora and there they came in trucks, bikes, hitchhiking, while the more enterprising ones from Klail leased a Greyhound that already had some people in it who had boarded the bus back in Bascom, and they too joined the crowd.

Three candy men appeared and immediately opened up shop: it was a hot one, and they started selling snow cones left and right. The crowd was later estimated, quite conservatively, I thought, at some four thousand. Some didn't know who was being buried. Most didn't care, of course, had never heard of Cano, but you know how things usually turn out: people'll use anything for an excuse to get out of the house.

As for Don Pedro, well, he had to take it, and he came through with no less than three hundred Our Fathers, between Hail Marys, Hail Holy Queens, etc. And, when he began to cry (anger, hysteria, hunger) the crowd understood, or thought it did: they dedicated *their* prayers to Don Pedro and to Don Pedro's dear, departed friend, the respectable what's-his-name. At this juncture, up jumped the orators again having gotten their respective second winds, and each repeated their eulogies and then they began to compete with one another until a time limit was set; this helped to settle them down.

The candy men couldn't keep up with the demand, and each one ordered another hundred pounds of ice; the ice company charged more for delivery and thus the price increase was passed on to the consumer who was not getting any more syrup, the candy men having run out almost from the start. It mattered little since the people didn't care, and one could hear the chant for blocks around: ice, ice, ice, they cried.

Not to be outdone, the choirs, having run through all their songs and hymns, sensed a God-given opportunity and crossed the line to join forces with the others, and the first thing you know, they broke out with *Tanturn Ergo* which was out of place and worse, "Come, Good Shepherd, Celestial Redeemer . . . " heard only around Easter time. Finally, the four groups began taking requests.

Now, despite the heat, the dust, the pushing and the shoving, the crowd behaved itself, considering; there were some frayed nerves here and there, and more shouting than necessary and then there were those thirty-four who fainted, but, all in all, it was a first class funeral.

As it turned out, about the only person missing from all this was Melitón Burnias. As he said, days later: "I was quite busy on some personal business, and I was unable to get away to give Bruno a proper farewell. I, ah, well . . . ah, you know, it . . . "

Almost everyone pretended they had no idea what it was he was mumbling about, and let it go at that.

Rafe Buenrostro

Delineations for a first portrait with sketches and photographs (individually and severally)

Chano Ortega, born and raised in Klail City, died of abdominal wounds received in June 1944, during the invasion of France. A quarter of a century later, his mother, Tina Ruiz de Ortega, walks the streets of Klail with no idea what it was her son was doing, as she says, "in those Europes over there."

What follows is for them and for a select few.

Miss Moy, our first-grade teacher, a mass of red hair and freckles hated it at First Ward School; she was forever washing and soaking her hands in alcohol and then drying them off with disposable napkins. Somehow she managed to teach me to read.

The next year we were transferred to Miss Bunn's room where quiet and sullen inactivity were the order of the day, and with everyday's routine being the same. One day, she decided to ask Lucy Ramírez what it was she had for breakfast that morning: and Lucy, trying to please, lied:

"Orange juice, Miss Bunn, with buttered toast and jelly, and two scrambled eggs." I looked at the free book covers they gave us: she was reading What Every Young Child Should Eat for Breakfast. Poor thing.

"Thank you, Lucy. And you, Leo? Did you have the same?"

Leo Pumarejo looked at Lucy and then smiled at Miss Bunn: "No, Miss Bunn, what I ate for breakfast was one flour tortilla WITH PLENTY OF PEANUT BUTTER!

Hilario Borrego, he lived in another section of Klail City, either bumped or pushed me, and when I got up: I bloodied his nose for him. It happened during recess when Leo and I had taken over the slide. If you came from our neighborhood, up you went; if you weren't, you were out of luck. It was a short, one-punch fight, but someone told his mother; the next day, during recess again, she walked across the yard and slapped me flush in the face.

I was seven then, and I remember that I cried for a long time. But, it was a personal affair: I didn't say a word at home. The rest of the year, though, I went after Hilario while Leo kept an eye out for the old hag.

Times were hard and things were bad.

When a city employee came to the Ponce household to shut their water lines, several families came to see what that was all about. The city employee tried to smile his way through, and looking at Doña Trini Ponce, he blurted out three or four words in some very broken Spanish. Doña Trini wasn't having any, and looking straight at him, she recommended he gargle with a glass full of bird droppings.

Life is fairly cheap in Flora, and if you're a Texas mexicano, it's even cheaper than that: Van Meers shot young Ambrosio Mora on a bright, cloudless afternoon, and in front of no less than fifteen witnesses.

It took the People of the State of Texas some five years to prepare the case against him, and when it did, the State witnesses spoke on behalf of Van Meers and against the victim.

In the Valley, the few Lebanese who live there are called "arabs" for want of a better name. One of these Arabs had a fruit stand, and every night he'd pick a few of us to move some 200 bushels of fresh fruit away from the sidewalk and into his store. And you know how he paid us? With rotten fruit, that's how.

The man was a son-of-a-bitch, of course, but what made it worse was that damfools that we were, we never complained.

In Edgerton, a man armed with a knife lunged at my father and me; we had no idea who he was, but my father then shot at the man. On the way to Klail City long after statements and etc., my father told me not to say anything about the incident right away; the news would get known at home soon enough.

We arrived, and I didn't say a word; trouble was that it wasn't long before I developed a stammer and, soon after, I came up with a very high fever. Had it not been for Auntie Panchita and her prayers, I might have never recovered.

Tacha was a very old woman who lived in the alley behind our home; when she died, my cousin Jehú and I went to see her. There was no one in attendance when we got there, and we could see and smell the cotton swabs in her ears, mouth and nostrils.

Jehú said he was brave enough to touch her, and he did. Standing there, he reached into his back pocket, and pulled out an old Indian head penny. He held it between his thumb and index finger and made the sign of the cross across her body; it's a good luck penny now, he said.

Pius V Reyes was buried in the mexicano Protestant cemetery just east of Bascom. I can't recall why my father took me with him, but he did; and it was cold, too cold for October in the Valley, I thought. We drove back to Bascom, and he took me to a house owned by some relatives I'd never met; I was served flank steak, flour tortillas and my very first cup of coffee. Ranch style, they said: instead of sugar, they used Karo syrup and no cream.

As I sat there on a straight chair, the women present took turns placing the palms of their hands on my face to ward off, they said, *el mal de ojo,* the eye of evilness.

I didn't believe in the curse of the evil eye, but ever since Aunt Panchita had cured me of fright and dread, I went along . . . I didn't know *what* to believe.

Aside from a public library and a stopped-up swimming pool, there were two cafés on Ruffing's main street along with some beat up buildings. One of the cafés didn't allow Texas mexicanos in while the other one did; now, it could be that the first would allow us entry but no service which comes to the very same thing. My father and I were in the second one when I spotted a black family, man and wife, and two boys just about or a little over my own age. Dad turned to me and said that black folks would only be served in the kitchen, if there. I didn't understand that part of it, and he repeated once and then again.

On the way home, I wondered how the black man had first explained it to his own kids when they entered the kitchen for service.

One afternoon, after school, Jehú and I were so very busy talking and listening to one another that neither one of us noticed a man walking the white line in the middle of the street; he was carrying a twenty-four-pound sack of wheat flour. As we came up, he stopped, wheeled around, ran and then threw the sack at us. Later on we learned that apart from being drunk, the man had been smoking marihuana cigars and cigarettes all afternoon.

Along those lines, a neighborhood boy, older, but not much older than either Jehú or I, became insane. The family owned a printing shop and, during the day, kept him inside their home, in the rear of the shop. He escaped by breaking a window, and I happened to run into him on my way back from a grocery errand; I was carrying a milk bottle, and when I saw him, I dropped the bottle and ran so hard and so fast, I ran past my own house. For a long while after that, I'd go out of my way to do all of the house chores, and I'd even invent some; anything. Anything, but run errands to the grocery store.

In Monon, Indiana, on the left hand side of Route 421 going north, there's a roadside place called Myrtle's, about two and a half blocks from a Shell station; we always stopped there to gas up on the way to Benton Harbor during the cherry picking season. When we stopped at the Shell station, Dad and I would then walk from there to Myrtle's for some doughnuts. Once, while the woman waited on us, she told my Dad that I was getting to be a little man now. Back in the truck once again, Dad turned to me and said, "This makes the sixth time you've made the trip to Michigan, son."

About a year after my father was killed, we received a formal *esquela,* a printed death notice; it was a woman who had died in Ruffing. I was going on eleven at the time, and I had no idea who she was. My two brothers and I went to the funeral, and although Ma didn't attend, she said *we* had to; an obligation, she said. On the way to Ruffing, my brother Israel, looking straight ahead, said that the dead woman was a half-sister of ours; our father's daughter by another woman.

I didn't know what to say; I looked at Aaron and then at Israel. Nothing. Knowing Dad as well as I did or had, and knowing Ma, too, I realized that, somehow or other, I had lived some ten years among strangers. And, when we arrived at the wake, the people there walked the length of the room, shook our hands individually as we each said and repeated the formulaic phrase of condolence, again individually; this done, we were given their chairs on the front row for the remainder of the wake.

Get some ice, hurry! Quickly now—on the forehead; yes. There, that should help stop the bleeding. No, no, you're going to have to tilt his head back a bit more, but be careful he doesn't choke, now. And you? What are you doing just standing there? Don't you see the shape your little brother is in? I was right all along, I remember telling your father that you were much too young for a driver's license. You go straight home, young man, and wait for us there.

Up front, ladies! Front! Here come the first customers of the day, two young American gentlemen to see us.

Gentlemen? Americans? Shoot, it was just Monche Rivera and me, and we were going on sixteen at the time; the one I got—or the other way round—wore a light cotton dress you could see through; this was my first visit there, and I was game but scared.

In Korea, out in the field anyway, powdered rations came in two flavors; after twelve straight days out there, Cayo Díaz, mess kit in hand, walked over from his tank to ours, and said: "We get powdered eggs and potatoes for early chow; we get powdered potatoes and eggs for mid-chow and, then, for late chow, we get a choice of eggs or potatoes. But I got me a plan. Listen to this: Tomorrow, I'm not going to eat this shit. No, sir. This boy isn't going to clean his plate. And you want to know what's going to happen if I don't clean my plate? It means some Chink'll starve to death, at least that's what they used to say at home all the time. Well, I figure that if I keep this up long enough, why, I can win the goddam war all by myself."

Cayo Díaz and a kid named Balderas and I went on our first Rest and Recuperation to Japan; the Southern guys in the outfit called them I and I for intercourse and intoxication . . . At that time, our recon unit was attached to the Triple Nickle, 555 Field Artillery Bn (Major Oscar Warren, Commanding), but we always hung around together.

We started drinking in Tokyo and somehow wound up in Kobe a couple of days later. At the Kobe Station we looked like hell, and a man approached us and gave us a card with an address; we followed him, and it turned out to be a geisha house. The man was a World War II vet, and he wore the light khaki uniform with billed cap; his prosthetic leg was made of aluminum or tin, and he played an old Hoerner accordion.

Before we walked into the place, we passed him forty dollars and told a woman there to tell him to come back the next day.

We had some Asahi beer, opened up the barracks bags and had our stuff washed. We had some more beer, bathed and each got an "only" for company.

We spent a week there, and before it was all over, I wound up singing an old Mexican standard about strangers in an alien land.

In the Valley, there are families from around Klail, Flora and Bascom who have known each other for some six-seven-eight generations, and many are blood related, as well. In spite of this, when a young man from Klail, say, makes plans to marry a girl from Flora, a commission is charged to ask for the girl's hand. They become serious and solemn; the about-to-be-engaged couple is nervous: he sweats, and she fans herself.

Obdulio Yáñez, a relative of mine, lives in Relámpago; those who know him for what he is, call him *La caballona*—the he-mare. There's no such thing, of course; still, he answers to that when called for breakfast, lunch and dinner. The words "shiftless" and "lazy" used to describe him merely reveal the poverty of the English language in his case.

Sitting on a backless bench, cue in hand, looking out the window and waiting his turn, he asks for some chalk. Someone has just reminded him that Paula, his latest fiancée, has gone to bed with almost every man in Relámpago.

He chalks up, and says: "Relámpago isn't that big a town, you know . . ." He walks around the table. "Two bits says I make the nine ball in the middle pocket."

When Young Murillo told Don Víctor Solís he wanted to test Estefanita prior to the marriage ceremony, Don Víctor replied that he didn't raise his daughter to be no goddam watermelon.

This happened a long time ago, and Young Murillo still considers himself quite a card, as they used to say; trouble with that is that at this late date, he still has no idea how many times he's been fitted for antlers.

One fine October day, Pancho *la burra* gathered every penny, nickel, dime and dollar bet on the seventh (and deciding) game of the World Series and left for Jonesville-on-the-Río. The people from Bascom swore (up and down) that he'd get his if he ever showed that rat-chewed nose of his in this town. Again.

Three months later, there he was: mounted on a thin-tire, royal blue Schwinn with hand brakes, horn, twin baskets, etc., and ready to raffle off a radio or a chance on a bus trip to the shrine of Our Lady of San Juan.

As the Argentine once said: Really, now, one can always rely on people not to do anything.

In Bascom, people walk softly and carry no stick at all; they go about saying things on the order of: I. Behave yourself; 2. Keep it down; 3. Don't do anything that'll draw the Anglo Texans' attention; 4. Etc.

The bald truth is that our fellow Texans across the tracks could hardly care about what we think, say or do.

Here's something of what the A.T.s usually say: "Oh, it's nothing, really; just one of your usual Mexican cantina fan-dan-goes, 's all. They drink a little beer, they play them rancheras on the jukebox, don't you know; and then one o' them lets out a big squeal, and the first thing you know, why, they's having theirselves a fight."

See what I mean?

When the man at the bank shot himself, just about everybody from both sides of the tracks knew the reasons why. His family was provided for by way of trusts and such.

Now, when Chale Villalón, in his junior year, stole—and that's the word—stole a jersey *and* a football, everyone from both sides of the tracks learned of it in short order.

Our splendid Board of Education instructed a constable to arrest Chale, make him surrender the items and teach him a thing or two about respecting other people's property.

"Rafe, if old Echevarría shows up, don't let him have any more beer, 'kay? I'll be out in back."

"Has he been drinking?"

"Most of the day, now, and you know how he gets after a while."

"What shall I tell him?"

"Try and see if . . . well, try and get him to stop, okay?"

Echevarría opens one of the swinging doors, looks about and makes for the bar.

"Rafe, how's about a Buddy Watson?"

"Sorry, Don Esteban, but we're out of Budweiser."

"You got any Hamm's left? Hamm's is a good beer, too, you know."

"Yes, it is, but we're fresh out."

"And what about that there Lonestor beer, y' got any o' that?"

"Lone Star? No, we're out of that, too."

"Mmmmmmmmmmmm . . . And Yax?"

"Nope."

"Betcha got Flag! At least the one, right?"

"No, no Falstaff either."

"Well, what *do* you have?"

"All we got's Pearl."

"Pearl, huh? Well. . . . Bring her on out."

"Quart-sized Pearl, Echevarría."

"Well, that's a break! They last longer, you know."

"But they haven't been iced, yet."

"It's my lucky day, Rafe; why, a man can catch a cold with iced down beer."

A voice from out back:

"Jesus Christ! Let him have his goddamn beer!"

No sooner did Tome Fonseca conk Robe Cantu with the red and white No. three ball at Perez Pool Hall, than the guys baptized him anew; this time, they named him *Three,* and in English, too. So, in less than a month, he answered to Three. To tell the truth, the conking was a boon to Robe; face it, it's difficult as hell to rise above the crowd when one answers to Shit-pants.

"Sit on *this!* "

"Your sister loves it!"

"Yeah? Well up your nose with a limber hose!"

"Why don't you take a bite!"

And on and on it went, and it was all talk; neither one really wanted to fight. Now, if someone had laughed out loud or said something like, "Why don't you two just go to bed together," there would have been blood, and lots of it, probably. But they were lucky no one did, and they were let off easy.

At other times, though, some bystander's wise-ass remark has cost a life or two; these two were just lucky, that's all.

Ma's burial day. That's the third time I've been able to cry. In my life.

The man in charge of the Draft Board in Klail during Korea moved on to become the V.A. adviser; he was given an office in the County Courthouse basement. He advised me to sign up for a two-year course in boat-building; after that, he said, I could then use the remainder of my G. I. Bill in another form of carpentry: cabinet making.

He'd done right well—his words—without college, and it was his honest opinion I'd waste my time there.

Some adviser; some advice.

Leaving the Valley for a while; I've registered at the University up in Austin. It'll be a new town for me. Will it be a new life? We'll see.

Sometimes It Just Happens that Way, That's All

LIST OF CHARACTERS OF

Sometimes It Just Happens That Way; That's All
(A Study of Black and White Newspaper Photographs)

The Cordero Family	Baldemar Marta, his sister
parents	Don Albino (deceased) and Doña Mercedes
Beto Castañeda	Marta's husband
The Tamez Family	Ernesto Emilio } brothers Joaquín Bertita, their sister
parents	Don Servando and Doña Tula (deceased)
Amelia Cortez	Dance hall girl and prostitute
Romeo Hinojosa	Court-appointed attorney
Robert A. Chapman	Assistant District Attorney, Belken County
Helen Chacón	Acting Asst. Deputy Recorder, Belken County

SOMETIMES IT JUST HAPPENS THAT
WAY; THAT'S ALL

EXCERPT FROM *The Klail City Enterprise-News*
(March 15, 1970)

Klail City. (Special) Baldemar Cordero, 30, of 169 South Hidalgo Street, is in the city jail following a row in a bar in the city's Southside. Cordero is alleged to have fatally stabbed Arnesto Tamez, also 30, over the affections of one of the "hostesses" who works there.

No bail had been set at press time.

ONE OF THOSE THINGS*

What can I tell you? The truth's the truth, and there's no dodging it, is there? It's a natural fact: I killed Ernesto Tamez, and I did it right there at the Aquí me quedo. And how can I deny it? But don't come asking me for no details; not just yet, anyway, 'cause I'm not all that sure just how it did happen—and that's God's truth, and no one else's, as we say. That's right; Neto Tamez is gone and like the Bible says: I can see, and I can hear.

But that's the way it goes, I guess. He's laid out there somewhere, and just yesterday late afternoon it was that me and my brother-in law, Beto Castañeda, he married my sister Marta, you know . . . well, there we were, the two of us drinking, laughing, cuttin' up, and just having ourselves a time, when up pops Ernesto Tamez just like Old Nick himself: swearing and cursing like always, and I got the first blast, but I let it go like I usually . . . like I always do . . . Oh, well . . . Anyway, he kept it up, but it didn't bother me none; and that's the truth, too.

You knew Tamez, didn't you? What am I saying? Of course, you did. Remember that time at Félix Champion's place? Someone came up and broke a bottle of beer, full, too; broke it right backside Ernesto's head, someone did. Ol' Ernesto'd broken a mirror, remember? He'd taken this beer bottle and just let go at that mirror, he did. Well'p, I sure haven't forgotten, and I always kept my eyes open; no telling what he'd do next. I wouldn't step aside, of course, but I wouldn't turn my attention away from him, see?

Well, it was like I said: there we were, Beto and me, we'd hoist a few until we'd run out of cash, or we'd get beer bent, but that was

---

*Editor's note: This cassette recording of Balde Cordero's statements has been reproduced faithfully using conventional spelling where necessary. What matters here is the content, not the form. March 16, 1970, Klail City Workhouse.

it: none o' that cadging free drinks for us; when we got the money, we drink. When we don't, we don't, and that's it.

Now, I've known Tamez—the whole family, in fact—since primary school and when they lived out in Rebaje; there was Joaquín—he's the oldest, and he wound up marrying or had to anyway, Jovita de Anda. You know her? Now, before she married Joaquín, Jovita was about as hard to catch as a cold in the month of February. She straightened out, though; and fast, too. Then there's Emilio; he's the second in line; he got that permanent limp o'his after he slipped and then fell off a refrigerator car that was standing off the old Mo-Pac line over by that pre-cooler run by Chico Fernández. The last one's Bertita; she's the only girl in the family, and she married one of those hard workin' Leal boys. Took her out of Klail City faster'n anything you ever saw: he set himself up out in West Texas—Muleshoe, I think it was—and being the worker he was, why, he turned many a shiny penny. Good for him is what I say; he earned it. Bertita's no bargain, I'll say that, but she wasn't a bad woman, either. Ernesto was something, though; from the beginning. I'll tell you this much: I put up with a lot—and took a lot, too. For years. But sometimes something happens, you know. And when it does, well . . .

There's no room for lying, Hinojosa; you've known me, and you've known my folks for a long time . . . Well, as I was saying, Beto and I started drinking at the San Diego, from there we showed up at the Diamond—the old Diamond over on Third—stayed there a while, and we were still on our feet, so we made for the Blue Bar after that. We would've stayed there, too, 'cept for the Reyna brothers who showed up. There's usually trouble for somebody when they're around, and that's no secret, no, sir. What they do is they'll drink a beer or two, at the most, but that's about it, 'cause they only drink to cover up the grass they've been popping . . . But you know that already . . . Cops that don't know 'em come up, smell the brew and they figure the Reynas are drunk, not high. But everybody else knows; Don Manuel, for one, he knows. Anyway, as soon as the Reynas showed up at the Blue Bar, Beto and I moved on; that's the way to avoid trouble; get out of there, 'cause trouble'll cross your way, and fast. As for Anselmo Reyna, well, I guess he learned his when I looked him down at the Diamond that one time; he learned his, all right. But there they were at the Blue Bar, higher'n a eat's back, so we got out o' there, and then went on over to the Aquí me quedo.

That's really something, isn't it? I mean, if the Reynas hadn't-a showed up at the Blue Bar, why, nothing would've happened later on, right? But that's not right either, is it? 'cause when something's bound to happen, it'll happen; and right on schedule, too. Shoot! That was going to be Ernesto's last night in the Valley, and I was chosen to see to it: just like that. One. Two. Three. No two ways is there? . . . Although . . . Well, I mean, it boils down to this: I killed a human being. Who'd-a thought it?

It's funny, Hinojosa . . . I kind of remember the why but not the when of it all. I mean, I've been sworn at, cussed at, but I always let that kind of stuff go by, know what I mean? But then, too . . . to actually have someone come-right-up-to-you like this here, come right up to you, see, point-blank kind-a, and, and, ah, added to which I'd been drinking some and Ernesto there had been break-ing 'em for me for a long time, and me, remembering a lot o' past crap he'd dumped on me, and him being a coward and all, yeah, he was, always counting on his brothers for everything, so . . . there it was—we went after it. Finally. After all these years.

Later on it I think it was that Beto told me about the blood and about how it just jumped out and got on my arms, and shirt, 'n face, and all over . . . Beto also said I didn't blink an eye or anything; I just stood there, he said. All I remember now is that I didn't hear a word; nothing. Not the women, or the screaming . . . Nothing; not even the guys who came a-running. Nothing. I could see 'em, though, but that's all.

Sometime later, I don't know when or for how long, but some-time later, I walked on out to the street and stood on the curb there, and noticed a family in a house across the way just sitting down and watching TV; they looked peaceful there, y'know what I mean? Innocent-like. Why, they had no idea . . . of what had . . . and here I was, why, I'd been just as innocent a few minutes before . . . You, ah, you understand what I'm saying? . . . I'll say this, though, that talk about life and death is something serious. I mean, it's . . . It's . . . Shoot, I don't even know *what* I'm tryin' to say here . . .

Did I ever tell you that Ernesto—and this was in front of a lot o' people, now—did I ever tell you he cut in every chance he got? Just like that. He'd cut in on a girl I was dancing with, or just take her away from me. All the time. Over at El Farol and the other places . . . Well, he did. One other time, he told a dance girl that I had come down with a dose of the clap. Can you beat that? He was always up to something—and then something happened, and I killed him. Just like that. Not because of that one thing, no. Jesus! It just happens, that's all. One o'those things, I guess . . . Maybe I shouldn't've waited so long; maybe I should've cut his water off sooner, and then perhaps this wouldn't've happened . . . Ahhhh, who'm I kidding? What's done's done, and that's it.

Well, last night just tore it for me, though; he swore right at me—no mistake there—and he laughed at me, too. And then, like talking into a microphone, he said I didn't have the balls to stand up to him. Right there, in front of everybody again. Now, I had put up with a lot of crap, and I have. From friends, too, 'cause I can then swear or say some things myself, but it's all part of the game—but not with him. Ever. I didn't say a word. Not one; I sure didn't. I just looked at him, but I didn't move or do or say anything; I'm telling you I just stood there. Damfool probably thought I was afraid of him. Well, that was his mistake, and now mine, too, I guess. He kept it up—wouldn't stop, not for a minute. Then, to top it off, he brings one of the dance girls over and says to her, to me, to everybody there, that he'd looked me down a hundred times or more; looked me down, and that I had taken it—'cause I was scared. Chicken, he said. The dance girl, she didn't know what to say, what to do; she was half-scared, and embarrassed, too, I'll warrant . . . But she just stood there as he held on to her . . . by the wrist . . . I think the music stopped or something. I remember, or I think I do, anyway, that there was a buzz or a buzzer going off somewhere, like I was wearing a beehive instead of that hat of mine. Does that make sense? I heard that buzzing, see, and the hissing, raspy voice of that damfool, and then I saw that fixed, idiotic smile o' that dance girl, and then—suddenly, yeah—in a rush, see; suddenly a scream, a yell, a, a shriek-like, and I saw Ernesto sliding, slippin' sort-a, in a heap . . . and falling away . . . falling, eh?

Now, I do recall I took a deep breath, and the buzzing sort-a stopped and I remember walking outside, to the sidewalk, and then I spotted that family I told you about, the one watching TV. And standing there, I looked at my left hand: I was carrying that pearl-handled knife that Pa Albino had given me when I was up in Michigan.

I went back inside the place, 'n then I went out again. I didn't even think of running away. What for? And where? Everybody knew me. Shoot. The second time I walked back in, I noticed that the cement floor had been hosed down, scrubbed clean. Not a trace-a blood either, not on the floor, or anywhere. They'd taken Ernesto out back, where they keep the warm beer and the snacks, next to the toilet there. When Don Manuel came in, I gave him the knife, and then I went to the sidewalk, to the side of the place . . . I got sick, and then I couldn't stop coughing. I finally got in Don Manuel's car, 'n I waited for him. When he got through in there, he brought me here . . . straight to jail . . . That old man probably went home to see my Ma, right? Well . . .

Anyway, early this morning, one of his kids brought me some coffee, and he waited until I finished the pot. You know . . . I've tried to fix, to set down in my mind, when it was that I buried my knife in that damfool. But I just can't remember . . . I just can't, you know . . . And try as I may, too. It could be I just don't *want* to remember, right?

Anyway, Beto was here just before you came in . . . He's on his way to the District Attorney's office to give a deposition, he says. I'll tell you how I feel right now: I feel bad. I can't say how I'll feel later on, but for now, I do, I feel really bad, you know. That stuff about no use crying over spilled milk and all that, that's just talk, and nothing more. I feel terrible. I killed a . . . and when I think about it, real slow, I feel bad . . . Real bad . . .

I was wrong—dead wrong, I know; but if Ernesto was to insult me again, I'd probably go after him again. The truth is . . . The truth is one never learns.

Look, I'm not trying to tire you out on this—I keep saying the same thing over and over, but that's all I can talk about. But thanks for coming over. And thanks for the cigarettes, okay? Look, maybe—just maybe, now—maybe one of these days I'll know why I killed him—but he was due and bound to get it someday, wasn't he? All I did was to hurry it up a bit . . . You see? There I go again . . .

Oh, and before I forget, will you tell Mr. Royce that I won't be in tomorrow . . . and remind him I got one week's pay coming to me. Will you see to that?

I'll see you, Hinojosa . . . And thanks, okay?

MARTA, AND WHAT SHE KNOWS*

. . . what happened was that when Pa Albino died up in Michigan as a result of that accident at the pickle plant, Balde decided we'd all spend the winter there in Michigan till we heard about the settlement one way or 'nother. Right off, then, that contractor who brought us up from the Valley, he tried to skin us there and then and so Balde had to threaten him so he'd do right by us. So, with what little we got out of him, Balde hired us a lawyer to sue Turner Pickle Company. He was a young one that lawyer, but a good one: he won the case, and that pickle company, well, they had to pay up for damages, as they call them. Now, when that was settled, we paid what we owed there in Saginaw, and with what we had left from that, well, we used it to see us through the winter months there while we looked around for another contractor to bring us back or to live up in Michigan while some work or other turned up. By this time, Beto was calling on me but not in a formal way. You see, we, Ma and I, we were still in mourning on account o' Pa, and . . . Well, you know how that is . . .

You've known Balde since he was a kid, and, as Pa used to say: What can I tell you? Ma's been laid up with paralysis for years, but with all that, she's never missed a trip up North. Well, there we were with other mexicano families from Texas, stuck up in Saginaw, Michigan, and waiting for winter to set in and looking for work. Any type of work; whatever it was, it didn't matter. Balde was the first one to land a job: he got himself hired on as a night man at the bay port there. Not too much after that, he put in a good word for Beto, and that way they worked together. Later on, but you know this, Beto and I got married. At that time, Balde must've been twenty-seven years old, and he could have had his pick of any Valley girl there or anywhere else, but because of Ma's condition,

---

*Cassette dated March 17, 1970.

and the lack-a money, 'n first one thing and then 'nother, well, you know how that goes sometimes. So, we've been back in the Valley for some two years now, and I guess Balde stopped looking. But you know him; he's a good man; he was raised solid, and no one begrudges the beer or two or whatever many he has on Saturdays: he won't fight, and that's it. He won't say why he won't fight, but I, Ma 'n me, we know why: we'd be hurting, that's why. I'll tell you this, too: he's put up with a lot. A lot . . . But that's because he's always thinking o' Ma and me, see?

Once, and just the once, and by chance, too, I did hear that Balde laid it to one of the Reyna brothers, and no holds barred from what I heard . . . but this wasn't ever brought up here at the house.

You know, it's really hard to say what I felt or even *how* I felt when I first heard about what had happened to Neto Tamez. At first I couldn't . . . I couldn't bring myself to believe it, to picture it . . . I . . . I just couldn't imagine that my brother Balde . . . that he would kill someone. I'm not saying this 'cause he's a saint or something like that, no, not a-tall. But I will say this: it must've been something terrible; horrible, even. Something he just couldn't swallow; put up with. It cost him; I mean, Balde had to hold back for a long time, and he held back, for a long time . . . Holding it in all that time just got to him. It must have.

And, too, it could be that Ernesto went too far that time; too far. Beto had told me, or tried to, in his way, he tried to tell me about some of the stuff Neto Tamez was doing, or saying, and all of it against Balde; trouble is that Beto's not much of a talker, and he keeps everything inside, too, just like Balde does . . . As far as me getting any news out o' Balde, well . . . all he ever brought home was a smile on his face. I'll say this, though, once in a while he'd be as serious and as quiet as anything you'd ever want to see; I wasn't about to ask him anything, no sir, I wasn't about to do that. At any rate, what with tending to Ma here, caring for both of the men of the house, and you add the wash and the cooking, and the sewing, and what not, hooh! I've got enough to do here without worrying about gossip.

I'm not pretending to be an angel here either, but what I do know is all second-hand. What I picked up from Beto or from some of my women friends who'd call, or from what I could pick up here and there from Balde. I'm telling you what I could piece out or what I would come up with by adding two and two together, but I don't really know; like I told you, I don't have that much to go on.

Now, the whole world and its first cousin know that Neto Tamez was always picking and backbiting and just making life miserable for him . . . Well, everybody else knows how Balde put up with it, too. I'll say again that if Balde didn't put a muzzle on him right away, it was because Balde was thinking-a Ma 'n me. And that's the truth. What people don't know is why Neto did what he did against my brother.

Listen to this: back when we were in junior high, Neto Tamez would send me love notes; yes, back then. And he'd follow me home, too. To top this, he'd bully some kids to act as his messenger boys. Yes, he would. Now, I'd never paid attention to him, mind you, and I never gave him any ground to do so, either. The girls'd tell me that Neto wouldn't even let other boys come near me 'n he acted as if he owned me or something like that. This happened a long time ago, a-course, and I'd never breathe a word of it to Balde; but! the very first time I learned that Neto Tamez was giving my brother a hard time, I knew or thought I knew why he was doing it. I don't really know if Balde knew or not, though, but like Beto says: anything's possible.

Some girlfriends of mine once told me that at La Golondrina and El Farolito, you know, those kind-a places . . . Anyway, the girls said that Neto insulted Balde right in front of everybody; a lotta times, too. You know, he'd cut in or just up and walk away with whatever girl Balde had at the time . . . or Neto'd say something nasty, anything, anything to make Balde's life a complete misery. On and on, see? Now, I'm not saying Neto Tamez would actually follow him from place to place, no, I'm not saying that at all; but what I *am* saying is that Neto'd never lose the opportunity . . . I mean the opportunity to push 'n shove, embarrass him until Balde would just have to get up and leave the place, see? You've got to keep in mind that living in the same town, in the same neighborhood, almost, and then to have to put up with all sorts of garbage, why, that's enough to tempt and drive a saint to madness. I swear it would, and Balde's no saint. So many's the time Balde'd come home, not say a word, and drinking or not, he'd come in, kiss Ma as he always did, and he'd sit and talk a while and then go out to the porch and have himself a smoke. Why, compared to Balde, my Beto's a walking-talking chatterbox . . .

The Tamezes are a peculiar bunch of people, you know. When they used to live out in Rebaje, it looked as if they were forever into something with someone, the neighbors, anybody. I remember the time Joaquín had to get married to Jovita de Anda; Don Servando Tamez barred all the doors to the house, and then he wouldn't let the de Andas in; they couldn't even attend the wedding, and that was *it*. They say that old Mister de Anda . . . Don Marcial . . . the little candy man? Well, they say he cried and just like a baby 'cause he wouldn't get to see his only daughter get married. I remember, too, that Emilio, one leg shorter'n the other by that time, was marching up and down in front of their house like he was a soldier or something . . .

It was a good thing that poor Doña Tula Tamez had passed away and was buried up in Bascom by that time, 'cause she'd-a been mortified with the goings on in that house . . . I swear. About the only thing to come out-a that house was Bertita, and oh! did she have a case on Balde. For years, too. She finally married Ramiro Leal; you know him, do you? His folks own the tortilla machine . . .

Well, anyway, yesterday, just about the time you went to see Balde at the jailhouse, Don Manuel Guzmán showed up here. He said he'd come just to say hello to Ma, but that was just an excuse: what he really said was for us not to worry about the law and the house. Isn't that something? Why, I've seen that man dole out kicks, head buttings and a haymaker or two to every troublemaker here in Klail, and then, bright 'n early, one of his kids'll bring coffee to whoever it is that winds up in jail that weekend. I'll say this, too, though: the streets in Klail have never been safer, and I know that for a fact. Anyway, just as he was about to leave, Don Manuel told me that Ma 'n me that we could draw our groceries from the Torres' grocery store down the way. Don Manuel and Pa Albino go back a long time, you know; from the Revolution, I think.

Things are going to get tight around here without Balde, but Ma 'n me we still have Beto here, and . . . My only hope is that the Tamezes don't come looking for Beto 'cause that'll really put us under without a man in the house. Beto's at the Court House just now; he had to go and make a statement, they said.

Oh, Mr. Hinojosa, I just don't know where all of this is going to take us . . . But God'll provide . . . He's got to.

ROMEO HINOJOSA
Attorney at Law

420 South Cerralvo   Tel. 843-1640

The following is a deposition, in English, made by Beto Castañeda, today, March 17, 1970, in the office of Mr. Robert A. Chapman, Assistant District Attorney for Belken County.

The aforementioned officer of the court gave me a copy of the statement as part of the testimony in the trial of *The State of Texas v. Cordero* set for August 23 of this year in the court of Judge Harrison Phelps who presides in the 139th District Court.

Romeo Hinojosa
————————————————
Romeo Hinojosa

March 17, 1970

A DEPOSITION FREELY GIVEN

on this seventeenth day of March 1970, by Mr. Gilberto Castañeda in room 218 of the Belken County Court House was duly taken,
witnessed and signed by Miss Helen Chacón, a legal interpreter
and acting assistant deputy recorder for said County, as part of a
criminal investigation assigned to Robert A. Chapman, assistant
district attorney for the same County.

It is understood that Mr. Castañeda is acting solely as a deponent and is not a party to any civil or criminal investigation, pro-
ceeding or violation which may be alluded to in this deposition.

"Well, my name is Gilberto Castañeda, and I live
at 169 South Hidalgo Street here in Klail. It is
not my house; it belong to my mother-in-law, but I
have live there since I marry Marta (Marta Cordero
Castañeda, 169 South Hidalgo Street, Klail City)
about three years ago.

"I am working at the Royce-Fedders tomato packing shed as a grader. My brother-in-law, Balde
Cordero, work there too. He pack tomatoes and don't
get pay for the hour, he get pay for what he pack
and since I am a grader I make sure he get the same
class tomato and that way he pack faster; he just
get a tomato with the right hand, and he wrap it
with the left. He pack a lug of tomatoes so fast
you don't see it, and he does it fast because I am
a good grader.

"Balde is a good man. His father, Don Albino, my
father-in-law who die up in Saginaw, Michigan, when
Marta and I, you know, go together . . . well, Balde
is like Don Albino, you understand? A good man. A
right man. Me, I stay an orphan and when the Mejías
take me when my father and my mother die in that
train wreck—near Flora? Don Albino tell the Mejías
I must go to the school. I go to First Ward Ele-
mentary where Mr. Gold is principal. In First Ward
I am a friend of Balde and there I meet Marta too.
Later, when I grow up I don't visit the house too

70

much because of Marta, you know what I mean? Anyway, Balde is my friend and I have known him very well . . . maybe more than nobody else. He's a good man.

"Well, last night Balde and I took a few beers in some of the places near where we live. We drink a couple here and a couple there, you know, and we save the Aquí me quedo on South Missouri for last. It is there that I tell Balde a joke about the drunk guy who is going to his house and he hear the clock in the corner make two sounds. You know that one? Well, this drunk guy he hear the clock go bong-bong and he say that the clock is wrong for it give one o'clock two time. Well, Balde think that is funny . . . Anyway, when I tell the joke in Spanish it's better. Well, there we were drinking a beer when Ernesto Tamez comes. Ernesto Tamez is like a woman, you know? Every time he get in trouble he call his family to help him . . . that is the way it is with him. Well, that night he bother Balde again. More than one time Balde has stop me when Tamez begin to insult. That Balde is a man of patience. This time Ernesto bring a *vieja* (woman) and Balde don't say nothing, nothing, nothing. What happens is that things get spooky, you know. Ernesto talking and *burlándose de él* (ridiculing him) and at the same time he have the poor woman by the arm. And then something happen. I don't know what happen, but something and fast.

"I don't know. I really don't know. It all happen so fast; the knife, the blood squirt all over my face and arms, the woman try to get away, a loud really loud scream, not a *grito* (local Mexican yell) but more a woman screaming, you know what I mean? and then Ernesto fall on the cement.

"Right there I look at Balde and his face is like a mask in asleep, you understand? No angry, no surprise, nothing. In his left hand he have the knife and he shake his head before he walk to the door. Look, it happen so fast no one move for a while. Then Balde come in and go out of the place and when Don Manuel (Manuel Guzmán, constable for precinct 21) come in, Balde just hand over the knife. Lucas Barrón, you know, El Chorreao (a nickname) well, he

wash the blood and sweep the floor before Don
Manuel get there. Don Manuel just shake his head
and tell Balde to go to the car and wait. Don Manuel
he walk to the back to see Ernesto and on the way
out one of the women, I think it is *la güera Balín*
(Amelia Cortez, 23, no known address, this city),
try to make a joke, but Don Manuel he say *no estés
chingando* (shut the hell up, or words to that
effect) and after that Don Manuel go about his own
business. Me, I go to the door but all I see is
Balde looking at a house across the street and he
don't even know I come to say goodbye. Anyway, this
morning a little boy of Don Manuel say for me to
come here and here I am."

Further deponent sayeth not.
Sworn to before me, this
17th day of March 1970

/s/ *Helen Chacón* /s/ *Gilberto Castañeda*
_____ _____
        Helen Chacón   Gilberto Castañeda
Acting Asst. Dpty. Recorder
Belken County

EXCERPT FROM *The Klail City Enterprise-News*
(Aug. 24, 1970)

Klail City. (Special). Baldemar Cordero, 30, of 169 South Hidalgo Street, drew a 15-year sentence in Judge Harrison Phelp's 139th District Court for the murder of Ernesto Tamez last Spring to be served in the State Huntsville Prison. ETAOINNNNNNNNN

Cordero is alleged to have fatally stabbed Ernesto Tanez, also 30, over the affections of one of the "hostesses" who works there. ETAOIN SHRUDLU PICK UP

No appeal had been made at press time.

Lives and Miracles

Final entry in the photographic variorum

TRUE DEDICATION

After all's been said and done with, the world's a drugstore: you'll find a little bit of just about everything, and it's usually on sale, too.

Belken County Texas is part of the world, and so, it's no different; its people are packaged in cellophane and they, too, come in all sizes, shapes and in a choice of colors. Now, since they're human, some are brave, craven, loyal, treacherous, while others are sharp and still others are so dull that it just makes you want to throw rocks at them from time to time.

A close look reveals that some are in the picture of health while others go around coughing, spitting up blood and forever stepping in and out of bullshit and what not. The writer—this writer—without as much as a "by your leave" steps out into that world full of streets and potholes and usually winds up taking a picture of the Belken County fauna here and there. If he's lucky, a book'll come out of that. The trouble is that there's not enough interesting people to go around; never has been, not for everybody and not forever, either. There's always been a scarcity. Look at this: just how many Napoleons have we come up with so far? Or Hitlers? Or Jesus Christs?

Still, there are some people in this world who live in fear and tremble at the thought of committing some egregious social error: the wrong fork, the wrong wine or of discovering a spot or two of fresh urine running down the leg of a pair of freshly starched khaki pants. (Remember Mión?)

What happens is that these people wish to live perfect lives, and that's when I go to work, and, because of that ill-fated desire of theirs, they will never know the pleasure of passing out at a friend's wedding or divorce. No; there they are: clean, spotless, a box of handy-wipes at the ready and then, just like that, Death comes calling, and there they go forming a straight line down the chute where push sure as hell doesn't come to shove. As said, whenever I see these people, I go to work. I only wish there were more of them.

Up to now, then, we've only seen one Napoleon of note (one Romeo, one Raskolnikov); but the three share coinciding views: they each wanted something for themselves, and you have to ask yourself where the fiction of any of them begins or ends. I believe it's a fraudulent piece of business to try and dress them up with other names or with a change of clothing in the name of originality. You start dressing a monkey in silk and other finery, and you're going to wind up with one sad-looking monkey and little else.

Look, there's only one nickel in the whole world, and it's plugged, and everybody's had or will have his hands on it at least once. Trying to come up with something original is about as bad as making love to your wife when you're thinking about something else at the time. You have got to keep your mind on the business at hand; the cult of originality be damned. So, all we've got to work with is people, but God love 'em and keep 'em.

From what I've seen, originality's about as plentiful and as easy to see through as a dumb joke, and man's got more of both than he quite knows what to do with. What happens is that we're forgetful, that's all; and too, we're mortal. The truth is that we're all equal, and the truth also is that we're not all equal. It's galling is what it is.

Short detour. The curious folk who spend much of their allotted time on this earth giving advice, tooling around with scientific data, offering criticism and then going around explaining everything, have every right to do so since we live in a democracy by God. I wish, though, that they'd learn to leave us alone to enjoy or not to enjoy life as we see fit. After all, we live in a democracy, by God! It's a big place, and there's room for all so don't push or you'll just wind up getting shoved. Boils down to that.

What follows in this chronicle of Belken County is dedicated to everyone of that county's splendid population. It's also dedicated to their mirrors who look back at them, day and night, in shame and pride, in sickness and in health, until Death do them part, amen.

WHEN IT COMES TO CLASS: VIOLA BARRAGÁN

Pius V Reyes was buried in the mexicano cemetery, a mile or two down the road from Bascom, one unseasonably cold October day. It was a simple affair, and the rain that day certainly didn't help attendance. The mourners bunched up here and there trying to defend themselves against the elements, and the steady drizzle never did let up. As soon as the last shovelful hit the casket, the crowd wandered off in search of their cars rather hurriedly. In the Valley, and it's no different in the rest of the world either, death and cold weather usually gang up to ruin someone else's good time; since it happens so often, it's just too much to be coincidental.

The recently buried Pius V, despite his name, was a convert to Presbyterianism. A serious sort even as a youngster and growing up in Flora as he did, he was more serious as time went on, and by the time he was forty, he was as solemn as a goose. Some people are just born that way, that's all; they're singled out, you might say: You, there, you're going to turn out this way. You, over there, you're going to be this other way. And you, yeah, you—and on it goes. As always, man proposes, but the earth encloses.

"And how about, man develops, but the earth envelops?"

That's good, too, but no more interruptions, please. As I was saying: Pius V died at the Holiday Inn over on Route One, right by where there used to be a small colony of black folks; but that was a long time ago.

Pius V was not at the Holiday Inn 'cause he worked there, no; he was there as a guest. Pius V worked as a bookkeeper for Avila Bros. (wholesale & retail, we deliver). Pius V, when he heard Gabriel's blast calling him to join that great number, just happened to be resting a bit on top of Viola Barragán, a woman who some twenty years ago was firmer than tungsten, and who now, right now, is just about as solid as she ever was; one of life's minor miracles, you might say.

Pius V bought the farm in medias res, thus joining the silent majority as naked as the day he was born.

Rafe Buenrostro says that he, and he was just a kid then, that
he went to the man's funeral; from there, he said, his father took
him to meet some Buenrostros who farmed near Bascom. Rafe and
his father, by the way, were the last to leave the cemetery that day.
(The Buenrostros came to the Valley with the first Querétaro
colonists in 1749 with Escandón leading the first group there.
According to the late Don Víctor Peláez, some Buenrostros are
poor, some have a little salted away and others just fall through the
cracks.) Well, sir, as the people were heading for their cars, a
woman was getting out of hers and walked to the fresh mound of
flowers there. She was dressed in a fine, form-fitting, full-length
suede leather coat; the hat too was suede, but it was fur covered
and had a veil attached. She opened a good-sized patent leather
purse, took out a small handkerchief which she then begin to untie,
and when she did, she came up with a gold wedding band. She
looked at it briefly then she buried it in the mound; her gloves were
muddied up, but she didn't seem to mind that or the rain and what
it was doing to her clothes. And, she didn't break down in tears or
anything. A trouper.

Anyway, according to Rafe Buenrostro, Viola had become a
widow at age eighteen, just a year or two away from the second of
two World Wars we've had so far this century. She played the
piano fast, loud and poorly; it was also said that she wrote and sang
her own songs.

Her first husband was from Agualeguas in our neighboring
southern state of Nuevo León; he'd crossed the Río Grande as an
exile and opened up shop as a medical surgeon in Klail, and that's
where he died about a year into the marriage with Viola. It was his
own fault for taking that prescription made by an apprentice phar-
macist.

Before the year was out, Viola hooked up with Don Javier
Leguizamón; he owns those lands over to Edgerton there; those

were old mexicano lands taken over by Anglo Texans first and by the Leguizamóns after that. Viola was with Don Javier up to her twentieth maybe her twenty-first birthday; it happened that she was replaced by Gela Maldonado, but that's another story. Viola was jettisoned all right, but she was a good student: her eyes opened up, and she learned to see through people; obviously a valuable talent.

"And what about the time that you and . . . "

Please! After the Don Javier liaison, Viola married again; this time to a German national stationed at the Consulate in the Mexican Gulf City of Tampico, Tamaulipas. The man had crossed the Río on a two three-week vacation, and when he returned to Tampico, there was Viola hanging on to his right arm and to his every word, you might say.

From Tampico, the newlyweds sailed for India; Viola's husband had been promoted and his new post was that of first secretary to the German Minister there. World War II came along ruining a lot of plans and a lot of futures for a lot of people, as all of us know. But there was Viola, a mexicana from Ruffing, Texas, only daughter of Don Telésforo Barragán and Doña Felícitas Surís de Barragán, in India and married to a German national. The couple was interned at an English concentration camp just outside of Calcutta for a while. She was there alongside her husband until they were sent to the birth place of concentration camps: South Africa. And there they were until Oberst-General Jodl signed some peace agreements in a primary school in some obscure French town thus stopping that part of WWII.

Several years after the war, she finally made it back to the Valley to discover that Telésforo and Felícitas had moved to Edgerton. Not one to lose time, Viola pointed her nose and her car toward Edgerton and found them none the worse for wear: she bought herself a two-story house, moved her parents in, and then took very good care of the surviving relatives; these had helped the old folks during hard times, and Viola was just paying back. After this, she settled down or so it seemed.

The Valley mexicanos couldn't quite get a handle on what was going on inside Viola's head, and about the only thing they could agree on was that Viola had been gone close to ten years, and that she hadn't forgotten her Spanish during all that time. Chances are that Viola didn't even bother to learn German at all; to tell the rigid truth, some actions do speak louder than words.

Time marched on as it always does, and the Devil, that insomniac, delivered yet one more surprise to Viola: Pius V Reyes.

Pius V, seriousness and discretion, sporting a well-starched, long-sleeved striped shirt, had married Blanca Rivera; with no children to raise, Blanca took to religion, and so she and Brother Limón ganged up on Pius V to convert him to Presbyterianism. Pius V said it didn't matter much to him one way or another, and this way the Ruffing, Texas mexicano Presbyterian Church gained another adherent.

So, there was Viola settled in Edgerton, and Pius V had never even heard of her. What happend was that one bright Valley day, Viola with plenty of money and time on her hands, was making her usual run up and down the Valley from Edgerton to Jonesville-on the-Río when a red traffic light in Bascom brought them together: Viola was staring dead ahead waiting for the light to change when Pius V crossed her line of fire. She saw that curious face floating by and said, "I'm claiming that one as my property, and I'm doing it 'cause I want to; I don't need the money for food, this time."

And so, the Devil saw to it that Viola's car developed a flat right there in the middle of Bascom's main street; Pius V volunteered to help, and that's how the two met.

But the Devil's unions don't last long as a rule; the affair lasted about a year until that fateful day at the motel.

When Pius V keeled over at the Holiday Inn, Viola—Fearless Viola—pushed herself out of the way, sat at the foot of the bed, dressed as carefully as she always did, fixed her hair, touched up her face, glanced around the room and made for the door and then for Edgerton. Pius V was found later on by a maid who'd come to turn down the bed; she ran to the front desk, and etc. etc.

So he was buried in the mexicano cemetery near Bascom; his loving wife and other relatives prayed to the Lord to save Pius V's soul, and they recommended that He take good care of Pius V, sec- ulae seculorum, amen. The mexicano Presbyterians from The Good Shepherd Church over on Ninth were commended for all arrangements (floral and waiters) from start to finish.

"And Viola?"

Viola's doing just fine, thank you. She's fifty if she's a day, and she's got plenty of money and looks it, too. The burying of the wedding band was a touch of class; as Viola says, "No merit in having class, really; but it's Hell, if you don't."

THE OLD REVOLUTIONARIES

They're dying out. There's just a few of them left in Belken County Texas; some are out on the street, and these are the lucky ones. Others are less fortunate, however; they're prisoners in those glorious institutions, the nursing homes. There's only one way to leave those places . . .

Properly speaking, those old men closeted in the nursing homes aren't revolutionaries anymore; they're spent cartridges; water-logged ammunition that won't fire. It's like trying to fit Mauser ammo in 1903 Springfields: you can try, but it won't work. It's sad, but that's the truth of it.

Those who roam about and sit out in the park are free, but their numbers will never increase. There is one consolation, though, they know exactly who they are and what they fought for; identity, that overused word, is not a problem. So, they get together early in the evening and talk out the night, polishing, rounding the edges and corners of their stories; telling each other about "la bola" as they call the Mexican Revolution; age and memory don't necessarily go hand in hand, but they do remember, and every night they charge out as they did when they served as cavalrymen in Villa's army or under Lucio Blanco or in that rump group formed by the Arrieta Brothers. And the places are always the same: San Pedro de las Colonias, Culiacán, Celaya . . .

Those old men, and I'll mention but three, Don Braulio Tapia, Evaristo Garrido and Don Manuel Guzmán, were all born here, in the United States, but they too fought in the 1910 Revolution as did the Mexican mexicanos. The parents of these men were also born in this country, as were their grandparents; this goes back to 1765 and earlier, 1749. It may be curious for some, but it's all perfectly understandable and natural for lower Río Grande Valley borderers, as is the lay of the land on both sides of the border; and, if one discounts the Anglo Texans, well, the Texas Mexicans—or mexicanos—and the Mexico Mexicans—the *nacionales*—not only think alike more often than not, but they are also blood-related as they have and had been for one hundred years before the Americans had that war between themselves in the 1860s; the river's a jurisdictional barrier, but that's about it. At times, even *that* doesn't always work out. As Don Américo Paredes says:

> The Mexico Texan is one funny man
> Who lives in the region just north of the Gran'
> Of Mexican father he born in this part,
> And sometimes he rues it, deep down in his heart.

Other relatives stayed here, in their native Texas, during the Revolution, and some formed part of the Liberating Texas-Mexican Army—the seditious ones, as they were called. They, too, were revolutionaries, but they fought here, in their own country, in what since 1848 has been called the United States of America.

The apostle Matthew says that few are chosen, and he's right; it's the same with revolutionaries: and they're somewhat akin to mavericks, too; they wander about unmarked, unroped and unfettered. But time, the constant eroder, takes its toll on everyone, and that includes revolutionaries.

I

Braulio Tapia was born in the month of August in 1883; his place of birth was once called El Esquilmo, but when the Anglo Texans came down, they renamed it Skidmore; Braulio was raised and educated by Juan Nepomuceno Celaya, and later on, by a maternal aunt named Barbarita Farías de Celaya, from Goliad, Texas; the same Goliad where the officer who replaced Gen. Urrea executed Col. Fannin and some others during the Texas Rebellion, 1835-1836.

Braulio first showed up in what is now called Belken County around 1908; two years later, he married Sóstenes Calvillo, an only child of Don Práxedes Calvillo and his wife, Albinita Buenrostro. Braulio and Sóstenes had a daughter, Matilde, and she married Don Jehú Vilches, and they had one daughter, María Teresa de Jesús, who married Roque Malacara. Working down to this last generation, the land once owned by mexicanos now belonged, in great part, to the Anglo Texans. Some mexicanos did wind up with land, though, and these can be divided into two groups: in the first, the old settlers who fought the Anglo Texans in both gun and legal battles; and the second group, the sellouts who accepted the lands given them by the Anglo Texans as a dog takes what's given it for a job well done.

When Braulio Tapia talks with his old friends, he usually talks about the man who raised him: Don Juan Ene; Braulio was in seven skirmishes and in two major battles during the Revolution: Celaya, Guanajuato, where Obregón defeated Villa soundly thus forcing the Centaur into retirement earlier than expected; and, on Villa's side, at an earlier time, during the siege of San Pedro de las Colonias, where he picked up two or three bullet wounds; he can't remember the exact number; he goes on to say that it isn't important at this date anyway.

Through him I learned part of that old song that starts off:

San Pedro de las Colonias
  Whose bells off in the distance
Distance!
  Remind me of her and of home
Home!

Evaristo Garrido is related to Don Braulio somehow; I don't have all the facts as yet.

II

Evaristo claims bachelor status although he did have two sons by Andreíta Cano (she's from the Ruffing Canos): Pascual, who died in the typhoid epidemic of '16, and Andrés who was born retarded. Evaristo had a third child, a girl, by Petrita San Miguel: Natalia, who later married Sotero Garza Parás, a native of Cadereyta Jiménez, Nuevo León.

The Vilches, Garrido and Malacara families formed an unshakeable alliance in the defense of their lands (all original grants from the Crown). The first run-in against the Rangers—*los rinches*—was at the old Toluca Ranch, a Vilches family holding, hard by Relámpago, but closer to the old burned church. The second engagement took place at the Carmen Ranch held by Don Jesús Buenrostro, who was also called El quieto. The fighting started on a Palm Sunday and ended the following Easter Sunday. *Los rinches* stopped their harassment at that end of the Valley when the mexicano ranch hands started firing back at them.

At other times, and other places, however, the mexicano property owners lost both lands and friends, legally at times, and as a result of backstabbing at others. Those who died in these affrays died facing North and with their backs to the Río Grande; as they said, "We were born here, we may as well die and be buried here, too. Come on, you *rinche* bastards!"

During the Toluca Ranch shoot-out, some Mexican nationals related to the Texas mexicanos, crossed the Río to help out their blood relatives; they didn't fight, but their presence helped: they had crossed upon learning that some self-styled volunteers from the U.S. Cavalry had camped out close to Vilches and Malacara ranch land; the *nacionales* were kin, of course, and they stayed around watching the Toluca people shoot it out with the Rangers; it was a stand-off, and when the host packed up and headed for Fort Jones in Jonesville on-the-Río, the *nacionales* recrossed the Río and kept an eye on the cavalry's rear guard all the way to Fort Jones.

Evaristo, too, was in the sieges of both Culiacán and Matamoros with Lucio Blanco. During the shelling of Matamoros,
Evaristo paid a visit to some kin in the Yescas settlement—the
caserío Yescas, which is across and just east of Relámpago, Texas.
It was there that he met up with Petrita San Miguel. In Culiacán—
some time back—he didn't fare as well: an old Italian hand
grenade went off in his hand, and Evaristo lost the hand and every
finger that went with it, right there in the state of Sinaloa.

III

Don Manuel Guzmán met and worked personally with
Obregón and Villa. He started off by selling horses to Obregón and
wound up as a volunteer mine sapper for Villa. He left Villa, as did
many who lived through it, after the disaster at Celaya; back in the
Valley, he tried to settle in Flora but gave that up when he got to
know some of the people. So, it was back to Klail City, and happy
to do so. He spent a few months contacting other revolutionaries;
he also married there, paid some back taxes on some old land, and,
leaving his recent bride, he crossed the Río riding south toward the
east coast where he joined up with the Constitutional Army in the
Papantla, Veracruz, Military District. This, in great part, explains
his long friendship with Don Víctor Peláez.

Don Manuel married Doña Josefa Carrión, an orphan. Her parents, Julián Carrión and María del Pilar Sifuentes, were both tor-
tured and killed by some renegade Apaches during a raid at Seago
Point, Texas. Doña Josefa was a strong woman, and she loved her
husband and understood his ways. It's said of her that she never
listened or contributed to gossip. She raised five children: two of
theirs and three that showed up on the front stoop of their house on
a Holy Saturday afternoon, many years ago. She took them in, and
no one has ever learned why the three chose that house over any of
the others; the five were raised equally, and under the same name.

The man knew Obregón well and well enough to be named First Jailer in the Lecumberri Prison. He joined the Mexican civil service, life was going well, and he had made certain arrangements to bring the family to Mexico. This came to a halt when Toral de León shot and killed Obregón that peaceful Sunday morning at La Bombilla Restaurant. Don Manuel resigned soon after and returned to Klail City where he learned that Doña Josefa, strong will and all, had been no match for the attorneys and the land developers; a curious word.

But Don Manuel didn't quit; he went back to breaking horses and mules for the Tuero family. (There, at the Tuero Ranch, he had a run in with Javier Leguizamón. Don Manuel knocked him down and then kicked him out of the corral for good measure; at that time, Javier Leguizamón acted as hanger-on and messenger-boy for the Cooke, Blanchard and Klail family interests.)

Later on, Don Manuel operated a dairy farm, and ran three dry cleaning shops, two of which were in Flora and the third in Ruffing. He made himself some money, and he used much of it to help other revolutionaries whom he considered less fortunate. As time went on, Don Domingo Villalobos saw to it that Don Manuel was hired on as a constable in Klail City in the mexicano neighborhood. The Anglo Texans thought they had come up with a sop for the mexicanos, but the mexicanos themselves regarded Don Manuel, as they should have, as one of their own.

Born, as was Braulio Tapia, in 1883, the man, before his eyes failed him, could read and write Spanish easily enough; English was something else, and he understood enough to know that it wasn't for him. His lives, then, were all lived in Spanish.

His eyes aren't what they used to be, but he has something else going for him: friends and their loyalty to see him through.

A SUMMERY SUNDAY AFTERNOON IN KLAIL CITY

"Look alive! Heads up, Klail! Let him hit, Skin! Watch for that bunt!"

Arturo Leyva, bookkeeper, chimes in with: "Go, Big Klail, nobody hurt!"

Arturo isn't sure why he says *nobody hurt;* he thinks he heard it somewhere, and he's been saying it for years. This does not mean that Arturo doesn't speak English, au contraire. But the *nobody hurt* remains a mystery to him and to all who know him, and we should leave it at that; it doesn't always pay to go round lifting rocks since there's no telling what one'll find there.

The game's tied, and Arturo, up in the stands, takes notice that the third baseman moves closer to the line. This Sunday, the Klail City .30-.30 (The Thirty Caliber Klails) are hosting the Flora White Sox at Lions Park. The man up, a pinch hitter, is a fine bunter; Arturo, a keen student of the game, shifts his eyes from the batter to the third baseman. It's a tough game, too. Lázaro "Skinny" Peña is pitching a no-hitter in the first of a scheduled twin bill, as they say. (Skinny wouldn't give an inch to his own mother if Doña Estela happened to be in the lineup.) The Sox are up; it's the top of the seventh.

On Arturo's left sits Manzur Chajín, Lebanese by birth and candymaker and seller by profession; Lebanese or not, though, the Valley mexicanos call him "el árabe," the Arab. People know better, of course; they just don't care. Chajín lives in the mexicano neighborhood and is married to a mexicana named Catarina de León (That's Catarina with an "r" and not Catalina with an "l.") By the time they'd been married two months or so, Catarina was already a whiz at making peanut and pecan brittle; he also mixed peanuts and a fraction of crushed pumpkin seeds and sold them as almond brittle. For a while, anyway. (There's no trick to making peanut brittle; there can't be, not if those two are so good at it.)

Chajín speaks whatever it is that Lebanese speak; but he also speaks Spanish and, as a loyal Middle-Easterner, he pronounces his "p's" as if they were "b's", and says that Don Manuel Guzmán is a good boliceman and so good he doesn't need a bistol. Chajín has learned his baseball from Arturo, and in order to enjoy the ball games to the fullest, he hires kids to hawk the packaged candy boxes; as he says, "I'm the berson in charge."

Arturo went to the men's room during the seventh inning stretch; patting his tummy, he says he feels better, much better.

Baseball is one of the few indulgences owned up to by Arturo Leyva:

> Bookkeeping's his profession
> and baseball's his obsession.

Yolanda Salazar is Arturo's wife, but that's no secret; even the trees know that. Yolanda is the one and only daughter of Don Epigmenio Salazar, the proud owner of a king-sized hernia discovered— and left intact—just prior to WWII. The hernia is a bother, to be sure, but Don Epigmenio has other problems, other troubles and other social ailments that modesty and time forbid further mention here.

Arturo and his father-in-law have entered into a workable entente cordiale and are solid allies in a war of nerves (but never *words*) against Doña Candelaria Murguía de Salazar. (That's Murguía with an "r" and not Munguía with an "n.") The chances are very good (5 to 3) that Arturo has never read or heard of Dr. Niccolo di Bernardo Machiavelli (1469-1527), but Arturo is intuitive (a rare gift among bookkeepers) and he intuits that strength is forged by strong alliances.

The alliance is a rigorous one; and it has to be, because Doña Candelaria believes in despotism as a way of preserving peace and democracy. Arturo, for his part, keeps his eyes open and his mouth firmly shut. In re Yolanda, there's no trouble on that front: Arturo takes very good care of business, thank you.

On the field it's now the top of the eighth, and Skinny's hanging in there with that little screwball of his that he keeps moving around the plate: Not one hit (not even if Doña Estela, etc. etc.).

"Go .30-.30! Eagle eye, ump!"

"Arturo . . . "

"Well?"

"Nothing, dear, I . . . "

Here comes Don Manuel; the man claims no knowledge of this country's national pastime; he understands that it's a serious game, though. Don Manuel, as always, is wearing a long-sleeved white shirt with black tie; it's August, and it's hot, but you'd never know it to look at him. He stops, and the sun lights up the gold chain that runs left to right and back again from one shirt pocket to the other. A Swiss pocket watch attached to one end; both chain and watch are gifts and parts of Don Manuel's share and inheritance left to him by Don Víctor Peláez in his last will and t.

"ARTURO!"

"Yes, *sir,* sir."

"Yolanda just left, and she says for you to pick her up at your inlaws' when this is over."

"Yes, *sir,* thank you."

Arturo Leyva stretches his legs a bit. There . . . He loves Yolanda, but she's old enough, he says: she can find her own way home.

And now, Skinny's got his no-hitter in the books; the game's at the top of the tenth, and we've gone into extra innings. But there's a catch: the Flora Sox carry two Blacks on their team: the Moore brothers, Clyde and Mann, and there's not a better pitcher-catcher combination in the Valley. Unfortunately for the home crowd, Klail's .30-.30 is a team referred to in the game as *good field, no hit.*

Arturo works indoors; he's a bookkeeper, after all. But he's in good shape, and he's good for the long haul; tonight, for example, after the double header, he'll take Yolanda to the street dance on Hidalgo St., and from there he'll take her straight to bed. As said, he's good for the long haul.

I think I already mentioned that besides keeping Yolanda in line, he also keeps her happy; probably amounts to the same thing.

A LEGUIZAMÓN FAMILY PORTRAIT

The first Leguizamón arrived in Belken County after 1865; after all had been said and done with, as they say. Some wound up in what is now called the town of Bascom, and others settled near Flora; later on, some went to the north end of the Valley, toward Ruffing, while others branched eastward toward Jonesville-on-the-Río. At one time, they were about to join the Calvillos, the Suris and the Celaya families, but no marriage contracts were ever agreed to.

The proposed marriages dissolved and were forgotten. It was just one of those things. The second generation of Leguizamóns came and went, and they're the ones who grabbed the land they first nestered in. The original mexicano families said it was all right with them since there was enough land for everybody. A third generation came along, and lost part of the land, but the fourth generation got it back in spades and is still hanging on to it.

The first Leguizamóns were tough enough to hold on against the Southern Anglos many of whom came to the Valley holding a Bible in one hand and a gun in the other when they brought the Good News.

Clemente Leguizamón, the same one who was killed in Freitas as he helped the rinches in one of the first shootouts against the Vilches and Malacara families, sired five, and we'll talk about these here.

His first wife was the barren Carmelita Hennington who, according to the old mexicanos, was a quadroon; anything's possible, of course. His second wife was a not too distant relative of his: Diamantina Lerdo. The five Leguizamóns we're looking at, from left to right, then, are Leguizamón-Lerdo.

Diamantina died as mad as she could possibly be after being bitten several times by a rabid dog as Diamantina alighted from

93

her carriage after High Mass. This happened in 1904, the driest year in Belken County history. No rain fell in the Valley that year, and that included the extra day in February. (That same year, as a consequence of the long drought and millions of votary promises made to the Church at Klail, seven wains (*waínes,* as the Valley people still say) from Edgerton and Klail City jammed with people, rosaries and a priest or two, headed for a shrine in San Juan de los Lagos, Jalisco, to pray to the Virgin there so that it would rain over here, in Belken County.

(Julián Buenrostro, a younger brother of Don Jesús, *El quieto,* was born aboard the lead wagon on its way from Klail to Edgerton.)

The Henningtons left the Valley without a trace; they were there, and then: poof!, just like that, they disappeared. Talk persists that they went south, to Veracruz. The Lerdos came to the Valley in the same wagon train as the Buenrostros, back there when Escandón led the first settlers on both sides of the Río Grande Valley in 1749. They, too, were from Querétaro, but the Lerdos were a weak-blooded, watered-down lot: most of them died before they were fifty years old. (Reaching the age of fifty was the exception, really; the Lerdo union with the Leguizamóns helped the Lerdo blood somewhat, and then only as it concerns longevity.)

The Leguizamón-Lerdo family dropped the Lerdo end of it just prior to the Great War; the following identifies each member chronologically: 1) César died at age 45 in 1927; the irony here is that he was shot by those same Rangers he had sided with against the mexicanos during the early troubles of 1901-1903; the subsequent ones in 1915; and, the last serious one in 1923. 2) Alejandro, the tallest, a gambler and womanizer but no coward, also sided with the Anglo Texans; his reward was not an insignificant one: some eight thousand black dirt acres in Ruffing. Alejandro was found dead by the early crowd on its way to mass at the Our Lady of Mercy Church. Alejandro's head had been bashed in and his brains scrambled somewhat with a tire iron found lying across his chest. 3) Antonia. She married one of the rich Blanchards, and her sons and daughters, one by one, made Anglo Texans of themselves thus also dropping the Leguizamón tag to their name. 4 & 5) Javier and Martín, male twins, inherited the lands out in Edgerton. Martín was done in by good Napoleon brandy and a bad liver before he hit thirty; Javier, then, is the only surviving male, not as young as he would like to believe; his hair has the same color and consistency as that of General of the Army Douglas MacArthur, who now rests in p.

Javier and Don Manuel, when both were in their late twenties, got into a brief but furious scuffle. Javier bit off more than he could possibly chew, and, as a result, Don Manuel flattened his nose for him. This took place at the Tuero Family Ranch during the horsebreaking roundup. At that time, as now, Javier Leguizamón belonged to a small group of mexicanos who sided with the Anglo Texans. His early profits amounted to a fair sized chunk of western county land, as said.

Javier was married, and still is, to Angelita Villalobos, daughter to Don Domingo Villalobos; the same Don Domingo who personally brought relative peace to the Valley by meeting, talking, and convincing everyone that peace had to come, and that the time was now. It sounds simple enough, but Don Domingo commanded both honor and respect from both sides.

Don Domingo was not without a sense of humor, though: after a first, brief, meeting with his future son-in-law, Don Domingo insisted on calling him *hijo;* son. And, he always smiled when he called him that; it was the smile, you see, because what was left out was 'de la chingada' or 'of a bitch.'

As time went on, Javier added to his capital by branching out into the wholesale grocery business and, later on, added a chain of department stores. Jehú Malacara worked in one of the former as a stacker, price marker and messenger boy.

Javier continued his land trading, and he went after women in the same fashion. One of these was Viola Barragán, at that time a recent widow, and, among the Valley women, the most desirable. Another one was Gela Maldonado who milked him fairly often, and who also opened up a department store on her own. As the evil-tongued said, "Why not? She had experience along those lines."

It's possible that the history of the earliest Leguizamón may be of more decided interest than that of the above, but that's another story for another time. Of the five in this family portrait, only two remain as we have seen: Antonia and Javier, although neither has seen nor spoken to the other in years, as often happens in the very best of families.

Another point of fact: Antonia does not care (may resent, even) to be reminded of her mexicano blood, but let he who is without sin cast the first etcetera.

Javier isn't a mexicano at all, of course; the man is a Leguizamón, and the Leguizamóns, as is well known, are motherless; they were all given birth by a so and so.

BETO CASTAÑEDA

Dead at thirty years of age at his home on 169 South Hidalgo Street in Klail City, Belken County Texas, Beto Castañeda, married to Marta Castañeda née Cordero.

A hard and willing worker, he had five years of formal education, but he knew the earth, its products and the seasons as well as any academic who takes pain and pride to master his own specialty.

His parents died—were killed—in that often talked about train/ truck accident in Flora years ago; a Mo-Pac freight bowled over the truck and its cab, killing thirty-three of the thirty-six field hands who were on their way to the Schunior lettuce fields. (Before the week was out, the Ayala Brothers wrote words and music to a *corrido* relating the incident; the Acosta Printing Shop came out with over two thousand copies of sheet music for piano and guitar; this was then followed by a record cut by Águila Records in Corpus Christi.) Beto's parents were among those killed, as said, when the truck's engine stalled coming up the grade; it stopped in the middle of the tracks.

Beto was injured slightly, and he was taken in by the Mejía family; Beto enrolled at First Ward school (the mexicano school in Klail) the following year at age eight after Don Albino Cordero told the Mejías to educate the boy. As is well known, many years later Beto married Don Albino's only daughter, Marta.

By the time he was fifteen years old, Beto had made six round trips up North: one with Víctor Jara, *El pirulí*, Sugarman. *El pirulí*, on that trip, kept most of the money that the Skinner Produce Co. had provided for the migrant workers' food on the trip from the Valley to the fields of southwestern Michigan. The produce company sent the money to a bank in San Antonio; the truck driver, in this case *El pirulí*, received a check from the bank, and he was supposed to distribute the advance to the workers at so much and so much a head. He doled out some, but not all, then or ever; and don't think he returned the rest of the money to Skinner Produce.

Beto also made two trips north with Sabas Balderas: one on a cherry-picking contract to Benton Harbor and St. Joseph, Mich., the second one to northern Michigan—Traverse City—on another cherry-picking contract. The other three he made with the Cantú brothers' trucking firm; on the last and sixth trip, in his teens, he went up as an assistant driver: he spoke English better than most on the Tex.-Michigan route (Klail City-Texarkana-Poplar Bluff-Kankakee-New Buffalo).

Serious, somewhat reserved though not aloof nor pretentious in manner, he died of cancer at age thirty. His death does away with the last witness who, more than anyone else, knew the true, unvarnished reasons for that fatal stabbing at the Aquí me quedo a couple of years back.

The Tamez brothers, despite the death of their brother Ernesto, did not bother him in any way; now that Beto is dead and his brother-in-law, Balde Cordero, in the Doree Unit up in Huntsville Prison, Marta and Doña Mercedes Cordero are now at the mercy of the State of Texas.

To date, no one comes to mind as being Beto's equal in packing the type of vegetable labeled as thick and weighty: beets, broccoli, spinach, cabbage, cucumber and lettuce. Once, around age nineteen or so, he and Chale Villalón met in a *mano-a-mano* in a lettuce cutting and packing contest; Beto spotted him a case and a half advantage at the start, and they were to work four hours straight without a break. Beto caught up and then beat Chale by three-fourths of a case to spare. As far as Beto was concerned, though, the best tomato packer of them all was his brother-in-law, Balde Cordero. No argument there, he said . . . (Old Man Zepúlveda was the best all-around packer, and the old timers kept bringing this up, but Old Z. was a heavy user of grass and can be discounted.)

When it came to arm wrestling, there were only two men in the entire Valley who bested him; the first was Ismael Contreras, the all-time champ, and the other was Chago Lerma who was as tough right-handed as he was left-handed.

Beto was buried next to his parents at the mexicano Catholic cemetery in Klail; the Vega brothers were in charge, and Don Rosendo Estapa, who works for the Klail City Water District, gave the first eulogy.

Beto Castañeda, 1941-1971, one of a kind. R.I.P.

COYOTES

is one of the kinder names given to the fauna that is often seen but seldom heard in and around the halls of the Belken County Court House. They're not county employees, but they do nothing to discourage that impression: a white shirt, tie or, if women, high-heeled shoes and pantyhose. They occupy no office space; instead, they work both the halls and the innocents who come to that most inhibiting of Anglo Texan institutions, the aforementioned Papal See of Belken County.

They're not attorneys-at-law, either, but they speak, read and write English, are familiar with the simplest of forms, and thus enjoy a clear advantage over any mexicano who walks in with that well-known, long, white, window-addressed envelope.

The coyotes are also up on the latest gossip, and they enjoy another decided advantage: they're *sinvergüenzas,* absolutely bald faced types incapable of knowing or of being shamed by anything or by anyone at any time. So, when one of God's lambs wanders in, they're on him like stripes on a tiger. As said, the humble, who know nothing about anything, usually walk in with an unopened envelope: most likely the postman brought it that very morning, and off they go straight to the Court House; as the coyotes say, "It beats working."

Adrián Peralta, coyote, hails from Edgerton, drives daily to Klail (Sats. & Suns. excluded), is wearing an up-to-date, dressy, narrow brimmed hat, white shirted and an orange-white-purple tie (a tarpon fish miniature serves as a tie clip), his face smiling but his eyes not, a pencil line mustache, and, back to his eyes again, a yellowish-brown pair that have seen just about everything there is to be seen. In appearance, then, what the cognoscenti call 'natty' but in what he is pleased to call: good taste. His voice, mellow, without a trace of a nasality, which is proof enough that up to now no one's broken his nose for him. He is quite democratic, he says, and there he is, tipping his hat, nodding his head and smiling to one and all: the short and the tall; males and females; judges and cons; whores and pimps; etc. . . .

"Can I be of any service to you today, sir?"

"Well . . . I . . . ah . . . It's this here paper, don't you see. It came in today, in this morning's mail, in fact . . . and . . . well, I was . . . ah, it says Court House on it, see it? And, well, I just . . . "

"My name is Adrián Peralta, sir. I'm at your service and all I need is your name."

"My name? Oh. My name's Marcial de Anda, sir." Don Marcial who just sirred the coyote is over seventy-five years old, he's a candy maker, and he has three churchgoing bachelor sons: Juan, Emerardo and Marcial Junior, and one daughter, Jovita, who had to marry Joaquín Tamez. Mention of this last has been made elsewhere.)

"May I?"

"Please? Oh, yessir; here you are."

At what the Germans refer to as the psychological impulse, Peralta gives out a long, almost private, mmmmmmmmmmmmmmmmmmmmmm, steeped in mystery. (Artillery bombardment to soften the troops.) From there, he stares at Don Marcial and, before the fidgeting starts, another look at the envelope. (Reconnaissance patrols, radio and machine gun jeeps in working order.) And now Peralta opens the envelope and reads the letter. (The gathering of prisoners for intelligence purposes.) He takes Don Marcial by the elbow. (Mission completed, it's now a matter of filling and filing the reports.)

The pair go from office to office; people walking around, drinking coffee, some are typing, others stare blankly at a stack of papers on their desks—and on to another office and still another. Peralta looks at his watch and asks for so and so and then for some other so and so; no, he's not here. I don't know where he is. Thanks. Another office, and Peralta smiles down to the candy maker. (Good report, boys, we'll just send this on down to battalion.)

"This is it, friend de Anda. I'm going to get to the bottom of this, and I'll do it before you can count to three; and, speaking of three, you think you can rustle up three ones for me? It's delicate, I know, but one must grease this heavy bureaucratic machinery, if you know what I mean?"

Don Marcial nods but has no idea what the man is talking about; with the mention of money, though, he comes up with two one-dollar bills and a third one in change.

Peralta takes the money, keeps it in his hand and as he begins to walk away, he points to a small glassed-in stall:

"Right there," he says. "Now, be sure to ask for Miss Espinoza; you can't miss her: she's the one with the permanent and the glasses."

Miss Espinoza is a mexicana, of course. She is also something special: As she says, "I speak Spanish to the taxpayers, and the supervisors can go to hell and stay there." She smiles at Don Marcial and says, "¿Qué tal, señor? ¿Cómo está, usted?"

It's the tax assessor's office, and Don Marcial's name has come up on the jury wheel for the first time in his seventy-five-year existence in B. County.

"No, you don't have to serve right now; this is only a notice, Mr. de Anda . . . A notice; and it says that you may be called up during this session, but that may not come up until the end of the year, though. Here, keep this envelope; you come and see me on November 7—got that? The seventh . . . That's right . . . What? No, no, no; no money, we're here to help."

Miss Espinoza takes time to warn him not to go around giving his money to the County Court House Coyote Pack. Don Marcial nods.

Free! Home! He barely hears the admonition, and since he doesn't have to shell out his remaining dollar and seventy-five cents (it's four seventy-five for a candy maker's permit) he's already forgotten about the three he gave to the coyote. He'll also forget Miss Espinoza's advice: he's going home and in peace; until the next envelope.

Peralta's having his first cup of coffee at the lounge; it's a matter of principle: he won't drink coffee until he's had his first customer, he says. He's also on his feet in case, just in case, another one of God's lambs should show up. And they will. They always do, he says. And he's right . . . wide-eyed and lost, looking up and down, north to south, and left to right, east to west and then:

"Good morning, señora. My name is Adrián Peralta—may I help you in anyway?"

"Oh . . . Well, it's this envelope. It came in this morning's mail, and . . . "

BURNIAS

People. A fair-sized majority, I'd say, don't believe that it is so, but luck (and time and memory) comes and goes like the tides out in the Gulf. When it comes to luck, some have more good luck than others; some have less, and some have luck that is mostly bad; then there are those whose luck appears to be everlastingly bad and, like Mencken's ten-minute egg, beyond redemption.

Here's Melitón Burnias whose luck has been bad as long as anyone can remember. The trouble is, though, that he doesn't cut a tragic figure (Oedipus, Lear, Millard Fillmore) and so, those who know him don't sympathize at all; they merely laugh. It's a nervous laugh, but a laugh, nevertheless.

Burnias lives from day to day and tries to do so unobtrusively by keeping a low profile, as it were. To add to his bad luck, he lives in Flora, and the people there won't ever let you keep your own bad breath, as they say. Because of this, and his own bad luck, Burnias is up against it most of the time, and things then go from bad to worse and back again. Example (one and only one ought to do it): His oldest daughter, Tila, could have married in the local church, but no, she eloped with Práxedes Cervera, and here's what happened when they were back in Flora: they threw Burnias out in the street. Just like that. (This is the same Burnias who, on another occasion, and during a typical streak of bad luck, hooked up with Bruno Cano on an ill-fated treasure hunt.)

Martín Lalanda, Flora born and raised, is not an unlucky person; far from it, really. The man's a successful merchant, he owns some land, he farms on shares, and he is a former (but not too silent) partner of "The Gold Curl" barbershop. Lalanda also owns a truck; it's one of those flat-nosed Internationals which the Belken mexicanos call *chatos*. The truck is now mostly used to bring or, depending, to take gravel from place to place on a contract basis.

What follows, then, happened about eight years ago: Lalanda hired Burnias—as a favor—to drive that old gravel truck for him, but when the local underwriter got wind of this piece of business, he rushed over to see Lalanda, and said, "It's not a conflict at all, Mr. Lalanda. If you decide to keep him on, we drop the coverage; it's as simple as all that." (The truth, first, foremost, and always, was that Burnias had a running account with the Department of Public Safety; and the underwriter knew this, somehow.) Lalanda shook his head and waited for Burnias to drive up.

When it comes to money, Lalanda is, in a word, snug; but he is not a bad sort. (The oldest man with the best memory in all of Belken County is named Esteban Echevarría; and he swears that Lalanda has never bought as much as a bottle of beer for anyone, anytime, anywhere. Snug, then, but not a bad person.)

So, Burnias lost his job, and here comes the sky ready to fall on him again. But, to repeat, Lalanda isn't a bad person, and he knew full well that Burnias had no place to light that night, or the following, etc. Lalanda told Burnias he could sleep in the cab or under the truck bed. Wherever. And so, the truck went up and down in Belken County by day, and by night it served as lodgings for Burnias who washed it, cleaned and polished it, thus earning his keep.

It happened that one day Old Man Chandler—he's got some good river-bank land out by Relámpago—needed a temporary hand out there, and Burnias learned of it. He went to see him and was told that it was brief (3 days) and steady (16 hours a day). Burnias took it, started to work early on a Friday morning and finished the clearing late that Sunday night. After putting everything away, oiling the hoes and rakes and shovels and clippers, he cleaned out the barn for good measure; Burnias then went to the porch where Old Man Chandler, as luck would have it, was fresh out of ice-cold lemonade. Burnias understood, nodded and said he was ready for his pay. With that, Old Man Chandler nodded as well and paid Burnias but not in money. Burnias was paid in kind: a pig.

"It's a Duroc, Melitón; the best there is. I ain't got the money. All I got's the pig, Burnias; you take him."

Diddled again, Burnias thought. And so, he and his pig set out for Lalanda's International. The pig trailed behind him, and it was a sweet little thing, docile, which is usually not the case with Durocs, Poland Chinas or any kind of pig; pigs are usually bright and unusually mean. A tough combination.

Burnias was dead tired and dropped off under the truck bed; the pig did the same. At daybreak, Lalanda and his driver found the pair fast asleep, and Lalanda decided to wake up the one who could talk.

Explanations were offered, taken and then Burnias came up with a plan: "I need two dollars, Mr. Lalanda. I aim to buy me some corn for him there, and then give him as much water as he'll hold. It'll take a few days, maybe a week, but he'll fill out; you wait and see. When that's done, we'll sell him and make us some money."

Lalanda's ear pearted up on the *us* and on the *money*. He reached for his coin purse, and said, "Here's two-fifty." It went as Burnias said it would; that Duroc ate the corn and Burnias kept the water coming. Lalanda rearranged some of his thoughts in re Burnias; caught short, Lalanda thought he had come up with an up-to-now undiscovered talent in Melitón. Thursday came, and the two partners heaved and pushed Burnias' property onto the gravel truck and then drove off to the weekly stock sales in Klail City.

Lalanda went to park the truck, and Burnias led his pig to the disinfecting station. Burnias waited for Lalanda and once the Duroc had had his bath, the partners presented their pig to a young Federal veterinarian: thin, sallow, face full of brown freckles and matching sunglasses, he wore a white coat which came to his knees. He was a young one. The vet looked at the three figures facing him, and without a word of greeting pried the pig's mouth open and scraped its tongue. The Duroc snorted a bit, and moved closer to Burnias. The vet then walked around and bent over: he flicked at the pig's penis and the Duroc urinated into a flask containing some light green liquid; he kept his eye on the pig and said, "He's a mild one, ain't he?" Lalanda nodded and Burnias looked at Lalanda; the vet shook the flask and in a couple of minutes, the liquid had turned a deep forest green. Looking at Burnias this time, he said: "I'm sorry, sir, but this pig's sick. You can't sell him."

"No? Bu. . . . "

"Wha?"

"Pig's got worms in his kidney; it's a disease called Stephanarus dentatus. Know what I mean? Best thing to do is to kill him and bury him. Can't sell him."

Burnias and Lalanda looked at each other, and then both looked at the pig. Nodding, they went back to the truck and loaded him up again.

"I'm telling you, Melitón, your luck is *so bad,* that dogs'll line up to pee on you, you know that?"

Burnias nodded again, and said, "Yeh, I guess so; but why stop at dogs? Pigs'll do it, if you let 'em."

Lalanda, with no touch of malice whatever, laughed aloud and Burnias shook his head and laughed a while later.

"Let's go home, Melitón, the day ain't over yet." Lalanda started the truck, and they drove away from the KC Stock Yards. They drove without looking back and without a further word for the next half hour. Each rolled a cigarette, smoked it, rolled another and smoked that one, too. Finally, Lalanda coughed a bit, spit and said, "Tell you what, Melitón; let's you 'n me drive on over to Relámpago, and we'll sell this fatted pig to Old Man Chandler."

Burnias turned to Lalanda and shook his head. "But Mr. Lalanda, I got the pig from him in the first place."

"I know that, we'll just pop over and sell 'em the damn thing. Ha! He won't want to buy it—I'll say he won't—so you know what we'll do next? We'll give it to him; yeah; unload it right there, next to the other pigs, that's what we'll do."

"You, ah, you want to run that one by again?"

"Listen. The man won't want to buy it, but he can't refuse a gift, right? It's an insult. We'll just back up to the pig sty, is what we'll do. And since he can't refuse the gift—but if he tries—we can always ask him why? and if we do, what can he say? That the damn thing's got worms? We'll unload it, that's all."

"You think that'll work?"

"Leave it to me, Burnias. I'll do the talking."

≫ ≫ ≫

It worked; Old Man Chandler had his back braced against the fence there, but he paid the twenty-seven dollars Burnias had coming to him. Burnias took it, and Lalanda said, "We'll take 'em off your hands, Mr. Chandler, but it'll cost you five more."

Old Man Chandler pursed his lips, but Lalanda deflected that one; he reached into his shirt pocket and said, "Want to roll one while you think it over?"

Otis Chandler shook his head and forked over the five ones. On the way to the truck, Lalanda took the two-fifty he had given Burnias, and then an extra dollar: "That's for gas, Melitón."

That evening, Burnias walked into German Salinas' place and drank himself silly: he couldn't stop laughing, and he wouldn't stop drinking, and he stayed there until closing time not bothering anyone. The usual crowd was there at closing time; Burnias motioned to Germán and said, rather quietly, "Set 'em up for the boys there; and give 'em quarts if that's what they want." With that he made his way to the truck, but he stopped. He may have been thinking about his former sleeping companion for he hesitated and then decided to sleep it off in the watermelon patch, snakes or no snakes. Tomorrow morning he'd wake up with a hangover about the size of the gravel truck, but he'd have something at hand to see him through: a dewy cool, sweet, black diamond Arkansas jewel watermelon.

≫ ≫ ≫

I guess people just don't understand about luck, and that's why people are usually fighting, kicking, scratching and gouging; they should learn to hold back. When luck comes calling, people want it to be good, and for them alone; well, it doesn't work that way at all. It never has. Luck should be looked upon as a woman: sometimes women feel like it, and sometimes they don't. When they do, they choose the one they want, and the chosen won't be the wiser. He won't even know what brought *that* on. Luck's like that, too; man should not always heed the advice about seek and ye shall find. Advice is made up of words, not action.

DON JAVIER

"I've kept Gela in high style for the last thirteen years, and now she up and tells me that she and that dried-up sister of hers are leaving Klail; that they're thinking of going off to sell work clothes out in the ranches somewhere.

"And what's taking Jehú so long, anyway? Well, as soon as he comes in, out he goes again with another letter to her.

"Damn! Of all the dumb luck, and today, too . . . Angelita wants to celebrate our silver wedding anniversary. Why? Do people still do things like that?

"But it's my fault: I gave in to Angelita. I'm going soft in the head, that's all . . . A party celebrating our twenty-fifth wedding anniversary. Jesus! It just shows what a soft-heart will do. I shouldn't've given in."

(Gela is tougher than dollar steak; she's a terror in bed, on the floor, in a tub, day or night. They're not many of them left in that league.)

"No two ways about it: I know who's to blame for this change; it's that sack full o' bones sister of hers. And I know what *she* needs.

"And where in hell is Jehú, anyway?"

EMILIO TAMEZ

"That's Emilio Tamez over there; damn good thing he doesn't need glasses, 'cause you need two ears to hold 'em up.

"The man wasn't born that way, you know; he raised hell at Don Florentino's cantina one night, and Young Murillo just walked up to him and sliced an ear off."

"You mean, like a slice o' bread or something?"

"Yeh, just like that. And he's a gimp, too, and he wasn't born that way either. It happened like this: damfool must've been about eleven years old at the time, and there he was on the railroad tracks, jumping from car to car, when he slipped on a piece of broccoli, and landed on his knee. Damfool. They took him to a bone-healer, but it wasn't any use: that leg was meant to be shorter than the other, and it stayed that way."

"There he goes."

"Yeah . . . it's the law of compensation all over again: he limps on the left side and is deaf on the right. You wouldn't know it to look at him, but he reads and writes English and Spanish. A tee-total bilingual, he is; but, with all that going for him, he's still a damfool."

AUNTIE PANCHITA

"Who's sick, and where is he?"

"This way, Auntie, right through there."

"Goodness, it's Rafe . . . What is it, child?"

"Well, we don't know exactly. He started to stammer all of a sudden, and then he caught some sort of chill, and now, look at him: he's running that fever."

"I see; close the curtains and turn off those lights, will you? All right now, everybody out. Scoot!, and close that door."

Auntie Panchita took a brownish-looking egg from an ordinary grocery bag and made a sign of the cross around Rafe Buenrostro's face; after this, she made another sign covering the length of his body, and she began to pray:

"Prayer, incantation and psalm for the cure of the calamities brought on by fright and dread which afflict the body, mind, heart and soul, amen.

"God's own creature, I shall cure you and anoint you in the Holy Name of the Lord and His Holy Ghost: three distinct persons, but only one True God.

"Offering: Name the saints! St. Roque, yea, St. Sebastian, yea! Eleven thousand virgins, and all of whom and through whom, Your own passion and ascension will then deign to cure this creature so afflicted by the eye of the damned evilness, of fright and dread, yea!, and burning fever, which is reminiscent of Sheol to cure, I say, to cure *any other* disease, illness or affliction which You and no other, Lord, and your sacrosanct mysteries will cure, heal and thus alleviate. Amen. Amen. (Say Amen, Rafe! Rafe! Don't just shake your head, boy . . . Oh, well.)"

Auntie Panchita bent and made three more signs of the cross, and then repeated the psalm and the offering two more times after that; this over, she took and broke the brownish egg in a green-colored plate which she then placed under Rafe's bed. As for Rafe

Buenrostro, he took knowingly or not, a deep, deep breath and dropped off to a sleep which lasted a day and a half.

Auntie Panchita left rather hurriedly, as she usually did, anyway; saying she'd be back on Wednesday. Always the busiest of women: she made her hurried goodbyes to all, reminded everyone she wouldn't be available that afternoon, going, as she was, to assist at the baptism of Lino Carrizales's youngest, just recently born.

EPIGMENIO SALAZAR

This one owns a good-sized house with four rooms to let plus a further bit of personal property, to wit: a hiatal hernia that's allowed him not to turn a lick of work dating back to before WWII.

Epigmenio sees many things and reads a lot more into them; to add to this, those matters which he actually does not see, or witness, are then left to his ample imagination. In this way, he says, he doesn't have to go on inactive service—he keeps his hand in, so to speak.

For example, he knows what went on between the fry cook over at the El Fénix Café, and that youngish girl at the pharmacy, directly across the street; and, he also knows from three disinterested witnesses (best evidence) what it is that truly ails Young Murillo's newest wife.

Now, what *he* would like to know is how the hell he happened to come up with that fat-sized hiatal hernia of his.

FIRA, A BLONDE NOT HAVING TOO MUCH FUN

Straight on and from the shoulder, now: Fira is a whore, and she has been called that and more. In antiquity, Fira would have had other names: Alicaria. Caserita. Copa. Diabola. Foraria. Nocti vigilia. Peregrina. Proseda. Quadrantaria. Scrantia. Scrota. Vaga. A whore, then. But, a whore with a difference: she does not act like one (as housemaids sometimes do), she doesn't whore around (as the servant girls' mistresses sometimes do) and no flirting, no, not at all.

She has blue eyes, she wears her hair short and she neither dyes nor tints it. Her body would soon put a halt, for once and for all, to Father Zamudio's hiccups, or whatever he chooses to call them.

She's not from here either; she's a native of Jonesville-on-the-Río: the daughter of a mexicana from Jonesville and an Anglo serviceman from Fort Jones; she's neither the first nor the last of that kind, but, and the truth as always, she is a beauty. Simply put, then, the most beautiful woman in the Valley.

I'll tell you who knows everything there is to know about Jonesville-on-the-Río: that's Don Américo Paredes.

Our blond Fira is a serious woman who carries her whoredom as school girls carry their tote bags: naturally and with no affectation. And, after her daily bath, she smells of soap and water, and when out on the street, on her way to work, her hair, damp still, curls on the side of her face close to her ears.

My uncle Andrés has several illegitimate sons, and one of them, Félix Champión, runs one of my uncle's cantinas, and that's where she works; Fira doesn't dance and neither does she go from table to table; and she's not a drink-cadger nor a flirt. In short, she doesn't carry on and such. (Cervantes, through Don Quixote, once said that the go-betweens had, perforce, to be serious people of some repute for the good of the Republic; no argument there, but the whoring occupation in a run-down cantina of a still poorer town is no laughing matter either.)

114

The Klail City women know who she is, what she is, but they leave it at that; which is as it should be. Women, in the longer run, are a far sight more understanding in those matters; murmuring, then, is kept to a minimum.

Trouble is that Fira always faces facts head on; Klail is a town with a short supply of cash, and she's got to be moving on to Jonesville. Shame.

ARTURO LEYVA

When Arturo married Yolanda Salazar, only daughter of Don Epigmenio (he-who-does-no-work), he already had a job with Torres Bros., the owners of that two-story red brick grocery store.

Arturo is a bookkeeper for them; he stays out of his father's dog house by tending to the man's accounts for free: nobody's fool, Arturo also milks a bit here and there from various businesses run by his mother-in-law and thus Don Epigmenio manages to have spending money once in a while. This, of course, is done behind the generous backside of Doña Candelaria Murguía de Salazar, wife and particular cross of the Knight of the Woeful Hernia.

As is well known in the Free World, chicken pox lasts a little over two weeks, which is about as long as Doña Candelaria gets to keep help around the house.

For instance, she once hired Tere Malacara, R.I.P., and Tere lasted but two days: one with Epigmenio chasing her and the second with Arturo doing the same. Tere was poor, a bit underweight, but she was also honest; these are matters which too infrequently are found in one and the same person.

Needless to say, Tere told each and every one of the Salazars, again individually and severally, as it were, what it was they could do with their job.

DON MANUEL GUZMÁN

Erstwhile dairyman, a former owner of three dry cleaning shops, a one-time partner of a bakery shop and the ex-policeman of the Klail City mexicano neighborhoods *(vecindades)*. That was one of Don Manuel's lives.

Here's another: Peón, horse breaker, ex-revolutionary, he followed that well-known trail: Villa, Obregón and, finally, Deception.

Born in the Campacuás Rancherías (Hidalgo County), State of Texas, he was a Grand Master at three-card monte. He knew how to (and often did) mark cards, and he did it with a pin, at times a needle, dipped in the faintest red tint (it fades faster).

How it was that he came to be a lawman in the mexicano part of Klail is not known to this writer.

In another set of lives, he worked in the rice fields; as a gandy dancer; and, for a season or two, he herded sheep in Wyoming. Restless, but not to be taken as a sign of nerves, he was also fortunate in marriage: his wife, Doña Josefa, was at both strong and understanding, and who, from Don Manuel's own lips, "Kept those two partners in evil, the Church and the general populace" in check and away from their personal lives.

The man neither smoked nor drank, but could outcurse anyone in Belken County; also, try as he could, he never got the hang of suffering fools gladly or otherwise. An expert narrator (but not, alas, of jokes), his one weakness, if that, was spent on his five sons and daughters. The youngest son aside, he was fortunate to have seen the first of many grandchildren named after him.

His death, as some would perhaps neither suppose nor imagine, was a peaceful one; for a man who lived several lives, and some of these in peril, cold and hunger, a cerebral stroke laid him low and rather unexpectedly while sitting on the edge of the bed waiting for his wife to remove his high top shoes.

117

DON GENARO CASTAÑEDA, MASTER HOUSEPAINTER

Lucas Barrón, the owner of the cantina Aquí me quedo, is called Dirty Luke.

> "Prefers beer to water, does he?"
> "It's like he says, 'If it's so
> good for you, why do they go
> around blessing the dam
> thing for, anyway?'"

Among Dirty's regulars, one of my favorites is Don Genaro Castañeda, a Master Housepainter. Once, many years ago, this government called him to arms: We need your service in the defense of the nation against its enemies, foreign and domestic; furthermore, your services are also needed to preserve our way of life, liberty and etc.

It was the first of this century's World Wars, and the Master entrained for San Antonio for his physical (where a man in white sticks his middle finger up yours as a probe for hemorrhoids, or is it the prostate?). From there, to some military camp, the location of which has remained a mystery to this day. It wasn't long before he boarded a ship (under New York Port Authority auspices, one would think) and headed ever eastward until it reached France, where the fighting was going on at the time; of this, he is most certain.

From what Master Castañeda says, it wasn't so bad: He understood some English by then, he was paid just about every month, but with no idea where to spend it. Also, he says there was at least one hot meal every day, and sometimes two, or three, even.

He recalls that during a stand-to, he felt something tap him lightly on the forehead; he reached up, got it and looked at it: 'bout the size of a bee-bee, he said. He looked at it some more, and there

118

being no blood anywhere, he just flipped it in a standing puddle of water in front of his trench.

At another time, he did come up with a nasty scratch from some barbed wire, and this is how he spilled some blood on French soil. When the cannon finally stopped their firing once and for all during that first go round, he was put aboard another ship, westward this time, and then by train all the way to San Antonio. "They gave me some more money," he says. "And then, they gave me a ticket, by bus this time, and it brought me here to Klail again."

He's never left either Klail or Belken County since.

A peaceful man, the Master, as many other housepainters here, is a good beer drinker, or was; he says he never turned down whiskey, wine or whatever was available. It may be endemic to the profession. If that's the way it is, one should let it go at that.

He must be some seventy-five years old by now, but he still paints once in a while, and he'll have a drink or two, although this also depends on how his liver's acting up. Klail City probably isn't much different from the rest of the world out there, and so, he and his two best friends, Leal and Echevarría (they're all about the same age), talk about whatever it is that old men always talk about.

As for me, it was by pure chance I discovered that he was a veteran of the Great War. I was in Korea myself, and although we share something, somehow, I can't bring myself to ask, bother, perhaps importune him, most likely, about how it was Over There.

It could be, too, that what happened to him happened to me. It doesn't matter how much one tries to explain, one gives up trying to describe the experience. Finally, the realization hits that it doesn't really matter to anyone else.

The Klail City American Legion Post is a World War II product, and the name on the door belongs to Pfc. Joseph T. Hargan who fell, their very words, in the Salerno battle action. Chances are that these Legionnaires and their now weight-conscious wives, whose houses have been painted by Maistro Castañeda, have no idea that he was in France a generation before. It probably isn't important to them . . .

As he says, "The way I understand it, Rafe, for them to name it after me, I should have died over there. The way I see it, though, no honor's that big."

Here he comes now.

"Don Genaro, you doing all right?"

"Oh, hello, Rafe; yes, doing well, thank you."

"What can I get for you this time?"

"Oh, I'll take a Pearl 'n another for Echevarría, and make it a Jax for Leal."

"I'll take 'em on over to the booth, Maistro. It won't take a minute."

"Thanks, son."

Don Genaro Castañeda, Master Housepainter, makes his way to the booth; the pool players stop, nod to him in greeting, and I pick and choose the coldest beers in the house for him, Leal and Echevarría.

NIGHT PEOPLE

At sundown, our fellow Texans across the tracks close their shops and head for home; at sundown, on this side of the tracks, suppers have been downed, lights go on and voices are heard and names and words distinguished and spoken by the old, the middle-aged and the young.

"Well, I heard the other day that the Sooner Contracting Company from Ardmore was out looking for some hands . . . "

"I'm not sure, but I hear that Sugarman, you know, Víctor Jara . . . well, I heard that he was one of the subcontractors."

"Jara? *El pirulí?* Why, I wouldn't go across the street with that guy, let alone the whole damn state . . . "

"Tag! Let's play . . . "

"Kids, we can't hear ourselves talk; why don't you all go play across the way."

"Tag, you guys. Come on! That hydrant there is Home Base, Sonny, and you're it; remember, a hundred by twos, and slow it down!"

"Now it's Lolly's and Thelma's turn to guess first the color and then the number."

"Hey, Joey, show us that shiner, come on, Joey. Be a sport."

"Let's see . . . four, five and that's it, there's no more. There's three jacks missing, but it's okay, we can use pebbles."

"Boy, Delia, you're always changing the rules, that's not fair."

"I'll *fair* you; jump in or out, now . . . "

"Where were you last night?"

"Mom wouldn't let me go out of the house last night, you know how she is sometimes. Did you really wait for me?"

"I was here. Till one."

"Were you, really? One? In the morning? And just for me?"

"Don't laugh."

"I'm not laughing, Jehú . . . come on, let's go to the park."

"And what about your little brother?"

"He's with that gang of kids over there."

"Okay, here give me . . . "

"Jehú, they'll see us holding hands."

"It doesn't matter; they'd say we were, anyway."

"Did you really hang around till one?"

"And what exactly did that school nurse say, Doña Faustina?"

"Listen to this: she wants us to have the boy's tonsils taken out."

"Oh? And why would she want you to do that?"

"Well, she says if we do this, then Andy won't catch as many colds as he does."

"Hmph! You know what it is? It's just more of that Anglo talk; they're forever saying things like that."

"My turn, now! I'm round, but I'm thin, and 'cause I don't rot, I cost a lot. What am I?"

"That's the oldest one in the book; come on!"

"Next! Me! Me! At my fattest, I don't weigh much, and I don't fatten on food and such."

"I'm the one that told you that in the first place, for crying out loud . . . "

"Okay, okay . . . here's another; it's a new one . . . "

"Well, I tell you this much, if you don't know the contractors, and they're talking Michigan and such, well . . . "

"He's right, you know. You got to play it cagey with those guys. Shoot, there's no tellin' where or when they're going to leave you high and dry."

"You said it."

"God's truth."

"And no one else's."

"Listen, dummy, you can't divide five by ten."

"And why is that, Smarty-pants?"

"'Cause one's bigger than the other . . . and that's why, Possumeyes."

"Kids! Keep it down!"

"The time, Doña Faustina, it's gotten away from us . . . Now, where did Adela run off to? Andy! Where'd your sis go, son?"

"She's in the park, Ma."

"Well, go get her now. Scoot! Doña Faustina, we'll see you tomorrow."

"God willing, Doña Barbarita."

And now, the people on this side of the tracks are going indoors. There's more to talk about, and there'll be another tomorrow, as usual.

THE SQUIRES AT THE ROUND TABLE

"Genaro, that boy looks familiar; who is he?"

"His name's Rafe Buenrostro."

"Buenrostro? Which Buenrostro family is that?"

"Is he Julián's boy?"

"No, his father was Jesús Buenrostro; the one called Don Jesús."

"Oh, I remember him; died young, didn't he?"

"Was he the one that worked Old Man Burns' land?"

"No, you're confusing him with Julián again. Don Jesús had some lands over by El Carmen."

"Over by where the Texas Rangers killed those ranch hands back in '15?"

"That's the place. 'Course the Rangers got theirs, too, later on."

"Yeah, but that night, they were armed, and the Carmen hands weren't."

"God's truth . . . I remember now: Don Jesús was called *El quieto.*"

"El quieto . . . Are you sure about that?"

"Sure I'm sure; boy, Leal, your mind's going, you know that?"

"And the other kid?"

"The one that just left?"

"No, the other one; the one talking to young Buenrostro there."

"Oh, I know him . . . that's Jehú Malacara."

"He wouldn't be one of those Relámpago Malacaras now, would he?"

"He sure would. That boy was orphaned early; let's see . . . his dad was Roque Malacara, and he married Tere."

"Tere? From the tent show? Really?"

"No, no, no. The tent show Tere was named Peláez, Don Camilo's daughter, remember? This boy's mother was old Jehú Vilches daughter."

"Of course . . . Don Braulio Tapia's son-in-law."

"Aha! Got it now."

"Echevarría, did you know Don Braulio?"

"I sure did, and I knew old Don Juan Nepomuceno himself, the one who raised him . . . I was a boy then, of course."

"The Malacara boy worked with the Peláez family and that tent show of theirs. That's part of the confusion. Don Víctor Peláez taught that boy everything he knows."

"I bet Don Víctor didn't teach him all that Don Víctor knew."

"I'll say; Don Víctor was a good friend, wasn't he?"

"Amen to that. Hey, we're just about dry here. One more?"

"How many have we had?"

"Two, is it?"

"Dunno; you sure it's not three?"

"Well! Look at who just came in. Don Manuel! Over here!"

Don Manuel spots the older men, brings a chair with him and waits for Rafe Buenrostro to bring him his nightly cup of coffee.

"What are you all talking about?"

"The usual, you know. Not speaking for you, Don Manuel, but we're getting old."

"Ha! Don Genaro, the four of us here can still go out in the woods and live off the land."

"You really think so?"

"I know so, Master Castañeda; I don't know of too many things the four of us can't handle."

"God hear you."

"Amen."

"Boy! Turn that music down a bit—you're going to have the neighbors complaining."

"Yessir, Don Manuel."

Coffee over, Don Manuel turns to the group: "Gotta go; I'll be over at the corner of Third and Goliad—you all need a ride, just come on over."

The *viejitos*—the old men, thank him, as always; and Don Manuel Guzmán, native born Texas mexicano, looks out into the night and cuts across Third, a side street in Klail City, a town much like any other in Belken County down in the Valley.

Estampas del Valle

Rolando Hinojosa

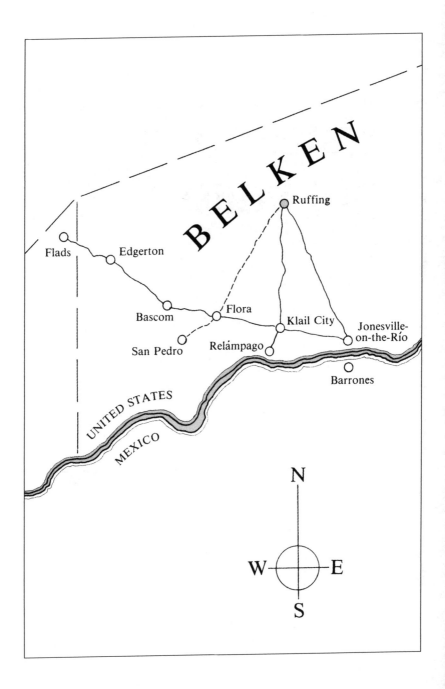

NOTA PRELIMINAR

Estas estampas son y están como las greñas de Mencho Saldaña: unas cortas, otras largas y todas embadurnadas con esa grasa humana que las junta y las separa sin permiso de nadie.

NOTA QUE SIRVA PARA DESPABILAR

La gente que aparece y desaparece en estas estampas, así como los sucesos que en ellas surgen, bien pudieron ocurrir o no. El escritor escribe y trata de hacer lo que puede; eso de explicar es oficio de otra gente.

Uno cumple con escribir sin mostrar la oreja.

BRAULIO TAPIA

Chaparro, fornido y pisando fuerte a pesar de venir con el sombrero en la mano, Roque Malacara me pone cara de vaqueta y dice que no es por falta de respeto pero ¿qué le vamos a hacer? no tiene padrinos y por eso viene a pedirme a Tere él solo.

Me recuerda que ya hace año y medio que tiene entrada en la casa y que ahora viene a pedir mi consentimiento para casarse. Le digo que sí, chocamos la mano, y le hago pasar. En el umbral de la puerta diviso a mi difunto suegro, don Braulio Tapia, con su bigote lacio y patilla larga, saludándome a mí como cuando yo vine a esta casa a pedirle a Matilde. Para ese tiempo ya estaba viudo de doña Sóstenes como yo ahora lo estoy de Matilde. don Braulio me dice que sí, me choca la mano y me hace pasar a su casa.

¿A quién vería don Braulio en el umbral cuando el pidió a su esposa?

TERE NORIEGA

Se me pegaron las almohadas; ¿qué quiere? Estoy con media hora de retraso . . . No es que me desvele tanto, no crea, pero una se cansa de trabajar y, si de veras le busca, pues, una se cansa de la misma vida.

No crea, habrá otras que están en peor situación que una; pongamos por caso a esas pobres mujeres que trabajan en las cantinas donde todo mundo las manosea. Peor: las que se van de criadas. Si es verdad que el peligro y el diablo no descansan, pues las que se van de criadas tienen que vigilar al señor de la casa, al hijo del señor y, ¡a poco no! a la patrona misma si se descuida. Sí, las de las cantinas y las criadas están peor que una pero una también se cansa. Si tuviera educación y fuera letrada le explicaba de otra manera pero una, ya ve, es como es y lo que sale, sale de corazón. Una se cansa y ya, ¿sabe?

ROQUE MALACARA

Mi Tere se cansa y con razón. Tenemos un hijo; amen del sue-gro, hemos perdido tres mujercitas. Mi suegro era un hombre cabal. Le gustaba la pesca y siempre procuraba que lo acompaña-ra su tocayito Jehú. Si la gente vuelve a renacer, diría yo que mi hijo y su abuelo son la misma persona.

HUÉRFANO Y AL PAIRO

Conocí la muerte y su finalidad cuando no había llegado yo a los siete años de edad. Ocurrió una tarde de tantas cuando volvía de la escuela: las vecinas no me dejaron entrar en casa y me despacharon a una banca que se encontraba cerca de la barbería de Gelasio Chapa. Allí lloré hasta que vinieron por mí para que me fuera a dormir. Por papá no pregunté hasta el día siguiente; me avisaron que llevaba dos días en la cantina de Cano y que sería mejor si no fuera a verlo. Así fue.

A mi mamá la enterramos no muy lejos de San Pedro y la visitaba cada mes con papá hasta que él, también, se murió así, de repente, sin aviso, mientras me contaba un chiste; un chiste que ahora, veinticinco años más tarde, todavía no me he podido acordar de qué se trataba. Cuando él murió yo tenía unos nueve años y tocó la casualidad que el día del entierro llegó lo que nosotros llamábamos las maromas.

Las maromas consistían de una carpa grande de donde se colgaba un trapecio, o donde estiraban alambres para que una muchacha en traje de baño o algún señor que la hacía de japonés o de borracho se fuera balanceando de una punta de la carpa a la otra. Por lo común había cuatro o cinco músicos que tocaban detrás de una cortinita que servía de mampara para las tablas donde un payaso o dos, o a veces, los mismos músicos, se presentaban para complacer al público. Cuando los músicos la hacían de payasos también vendían cacahuates y dulces en cajitas de cartón, no muy llenas, de caramelos verdes, blancos y colorados como el tri-color mexicano.

En otras ocasiones, otros señores, o quizá los mismos, porque eso dependía del tamaño de la carpa y del número de tripulantes, hacían chistes de la gente que vivía en el Relámpago o en el pueblo que estuvieran y todo el público se cagaba de risa (con perdón).

La cosa es que así que sepultamos a papá, a mí me dejaron solo esa tarde y no teniendo más que hacer fui a casa de la tía Chedes para ver a mis primos. Cuando la inútil de mi tía me vio, empezó a llorar y a hacer sus papeles. Por poco le doy la espalda y me pongo a correr porque, la verdad, aunque sentí mucho la muerte de papá, siempre le consideré como el hermano mayor que nunca tuve. Su memoria, pues, me era muy otra a la que se imaginaría mi tía Chedes y se me hacía que sus patatuses estaban demás.

Al rato se le quitó el llorido y se quedó con el hipo sempiterno; como la pobre era tan bruta, luego me preguntó qué andaba haciendo por la vecindad. Por poco me echo a reír pero me detuve y le dije que venía a jugar con los primos. En esto estábamos cuando de repente, la tía Chedes se llevó el dedo índice a la boca, y colocó la plancha en el hierro y se fue a la caja de hielo de donde me trajo un vaso de agua fría. Metió el dedo cordial en el vaso, me hizo la señal de la cruz en la frente y dijo: "Bébetela de un jalón mientras rezo un Padrenuestro al revés y hoy conocerás a tu nuevo padre".

Me le quedé viendo con tamaña boca abierta pero por sí o por no me empiné el vaso mientras ella canturreaba: amén, mal todo de líbranos y deudores . . .

MIS PRIMOS

Mi tía Chedes tuvo tres retoños de su señor esposo, Juan Briones. El primero que nació fue mi primo Blas.

A Blas lo bautizaron Blas Briones pero a los tres años de edad ya le llamaban Ronco y hoy día pocos de los que lo conocen sabrán su nombre de pila. De lo de Briones ni rastro porque es conocido que los sobrenombres, a veces, suelen barrer con todo: nombre de pila, apellido y hasta con el carácter del agraciado. También hay veces que los sobrenombres no encajan del todo bien y creo que esto se deba a que hay un poco de todo en el huerto del Señor. Como ejemplo de esto último les pongo a Antero de León a quien llamaban El Vivo. El cerrado de Antero era más bruto que hecho a encargo y lo poco que tenía de vivo era el color que se acercaba, de una manera alarmante, a un verde subido.

Ronco se hizo troquero y así que pudo puso al mundo en aviso: "El otro pedo que tire me lo van a oír en Ohio".

Los otros dos eran Eduviges a la que llamábamos Edu, que se explica fácilmente, y Santos, al que llamábamos Pepe, cosa más difícil de explicar. Después, a Eduviges, en la escuela, la llamaron Vicky; a Pepe, en la escuela también, le llamaron El Mión, algo que se explicaba al golpe. Allí en este último caso, el sobrenombre y la persona hallaron su perfecto aunque, a veces, penoso corolario.

A Mión, después de tantas faenas, el gobierno estatal le patrocinó un viaje de ida a la pinta en Sugarland donde, con aplicación y esmero, se adiestró a fabricar placas de carro. Es esta una profesión muy especializada pero poco rendidora, a lo menos para Mión, porque nunca logró ejercerla después que terminó su enseñanza en Sugarland. Cuando Mión volvió de la pinta, vino llenito de tatús y se convirtió en un verdadero espectáculo. En un colorido y entretenido espectáculo.

Con eso de llamarse Mión y ahora luciendo tanto tatuaje, la gente se despistó y no supo qué llamarle: si Mión o Tatú. Parece que a la gente no le gusta que la despisten. Por fin, mi primo fue el que puso pare a la discusión diciendo que prefería que le llamaran Mión. La gente, generosamente, accedió al gusto de mi primo y así Mión volvió a ser Mión.

La tercera, mi prima Vicky, tardó en asentar cabeza con lo que dio debida razón al dicho de que de tal palo tal astilla. Supongo que en Vicky el proverbio iría de doble bolazo porque mi tía Chedes era una perfecta güila galetera. Cuando Vicky le avisó a mi tía Chedes que dejaba la escuela para irse con una carpa de maromeros (que venía a Relámpago dos veces al año), mi tía Chedes lloró que fue un encanto: se desmayó, luego chilló, pataleó, se peyó, gritó y le dio el hipo; vamos, lo de siempre cuando se ponía nerviosa. Al fin se conformó; poniendo una cara seria, sentó a Vicky en frente de sí, y cogiéndole de las manos, le pidió que se cuidara de las malas compañías. En el segundo respiro, la tía también le pidió pases gratis para la familia. Pasando el tiempo, Vicky cumplió este segundo petitorio fielmente, con lo que, en parte, demostró lo obediente que era.

Del primer petitorio, Vicky misma, en tonos que mostraban su doblez jesuita, explicaba que había sido formulado en sentidos demasiado generales para que ella acatara con rigor y al pie de la letra. (A veces la Vicky hacía respingar al más listo con tanta lógica maquiavélica extraída de insospechadas venas de sabiduría . . .)

Cuando a Juan Briones le avisaron que él y la tía Chedes se quedaban solos, él tomó la noticia con notable ejemplaridad estoica: ordenó otra cerveza y otra docena de ostiones.

Hay gente que no le tiene miedo a nada.

CONTRATIEMPOS DEL OFICIO

—A ver, sostén el yaque así, de la manguera; pero con fuerza, Jehú, ándale, así. Ya está. Ahora, agarra la palanca (ah, como está chingando esta agüita) y jálale pa arriba y pa abajo para que pueda sacar esa llanta jija de su tuerta madre. Sí, no tiene ni qué, tenía que ser la llanta de adentro la del pinche flat.

—Cuidado que no se resbale, don Víctor.

—Gracias, hijo. No, no me resbalo pero de lo que no me pierdo va a ser de un catarro bien padre. Mira, ponte águila y que no se pierdan las tuercas. Estoy lo que se llama empapado.

—Estamos como dijo el otro.

—Cierto, Jehú, estamos. Y como dijo Cuauhtémoc, ¿eh? ¿crees que yo estoy en un lecho de rosas?

—Fue Moctezuma.

—Bueno; yo ya me entiendo. ¡Ándale llanta puta! ¡Sal!

—¡Qué sal!

—No, que le digo que salga.

—Sí, lo sé, pero qué sal la nuestra de encontrarnos a siete millas de Edgerton.

—También es sal; tienes razón. Dale un poco más al yaque, hijo. Ten cuidado, Jehú, que no se te resbale y te medio mate la mugre.

—No tenga cuidado, don Víctor. Usted es el que debe estar al alba.

—Ah, ah, ah ahhhhhhhaa ¡sal! . . . con una chingada . . . Ya está . . . alcánzame la extra.

—¿Le ayudo a acomodarla?"

—No, hijo. Mira, tente al yaque. Eso . . . (¿Y por qué no llueve más recio, Diosito?). Avisao, Jehú; ponte aguzao; pásame la espátula. Ya . . . El martillo. Ya . . . Ahora sí, aflójale al yaque poco a poco. (¡Qué bendición de agua y con norte para acabarla de arruinar!).

—¿Le sigo?

—Sí, poco a poco y cuídate que no se zafe y te quiebre la canilla. Eso. Eso. Ya está.

—Voy a ver aquel pedazo de lona que se desató.

—Cuidado con el tráfico que esta gente es más bruta que mandada a hacer.

Don Víctor Peláez tenía razón: el viento estaba poniéndose fresco, quizá demasiado fresco para octubre. Al otro lado del camión marca Internacional estaba Jehú Malacara atando una parte de la carpa de lona que se había desatado. El chico cogió dos puntas de lona y las apretó hasta que los anillos de metal estaban juntos, al instante los estiró hasta unos ganchos que servían, a la vez, como atadura y ancla de la carpa.

Los tenis, llenos de lodo, producían un cuaf-cuaf mientras Jehú andaba alrededor del camión para asegurar que todo estaba listo. No llevaba la cachucha porque de nada le serviría; el pelo rizado le daba un aire de angelito flaco con ojos inocentes y sagaces, levadura propia de la niñez.

—¿Qué tal? ¿Ya?

—Sí, don Víctor.

—Pues, trépate que ya es hora de que alcancemos a los demás.

—¿Qué horas son?

—No sé; ¿Serán las diez, tú?

—A lo mejor.

—¿Qué te parece si en vez de colarnos ahorita nos paramos en cualquier restorán y nos echamos un chorizo con huevos?

—¿Con tortillas de harina?

—Con tortillas de harina.

—¿Con una soda colorada?

—Con una soda colorada.

—Chingao . . . esto sí que es vivir.

El camión International carraspeó dos o tres veces al arrancarse rumbo a Edgerton donde el hermano de don Víctor les estaría esperando y creyendo, tal vez, que Víctor se había detenido para echarse un trago.

Jehú Malacara, acomodándose lo mejor que pudo, descansó la cabeza sobre la ventana que recibía la lluvia y los reflejos de la luz que los carros despedían al pasar. Se durmió sin darse cuenta.

APRENDIENDO EL OFICIO

—Mira, Jehú, vale más que agarres la cadena de por abajo, no sea que se suelte y te saque un ojo con el chicotazo. . . Ajá, ¿ya ves que fácil? Bueno, ahora me le jalas un tantito más . . . ándale . . . ¿ves cómo se afloja por ella sola? Ahora, estírale de la punta así y trata de encajarla en el poste muerto. Ya; ahora lo único que tienes que hacer es repetir la misma operación con estos tres postes medianos y cuando se llegue la hora, verás cómo se levanta una carpa de maromas.

—Don Víctor, ¿cuándo vuelven don Camilo y doña Chucha?

—No han de tardar . . . eso de conseguir los permisos para el convite y las funciones es cosa hecha, sabes. Camilo va con don Manuel, el empleado, y le dice cuánto tiempo vamos a estar, le paga el permiso, le da unos pases para el show y ya. No tiene magia la cosa. ¿Qué? ¿Ya acabaste? Bueno, ahora vámonos a la casita de los tíquetes para ver cómo va lo que te has memorizado.

—¿Me llevo la bocina?

—Dámela . . . este . . . ¿por qué no das los anuncios sin bocina; así, de pulmón abierto?

—¿Usté cree?

—Hijo, si no se cala la sandía no se sabe cómo sabe.

—Lo que usted diga . . . ahí va, pues . . .

Con la ayuda de don Víctor Peláez, Jehú Malacara se montó en un banquito azul celeste y empezó a tortillear tal y como lo hacía don Camilo cuando éste empezaba los anuncios.

Tanto la perorata como la persona eran innecesarias ya que la maroma consistía de una sola carpa y la gente vendría con el único propósito de comprar boletos para la función y sanseacabó . . . pero, según Santo Tomás, la fuerza del hábito la convierte en código riguroso y así es que sería impensable que no hubiese animador estacionado en frente de la carpa.

Lo que se decía, francamente, tampoco era nada nuevo y su mayor atracción podía estribar en el gusto de la gente que, ya es sabido, no sufre cambios sin previo aviso. Jehú Malacara se dio cuenta de esto por sí solo; con la ayuda de don Víctor se dio harta cuenta de mucho más, como se verá en su debido tiempo.

—A ver, hijo, empieza ya . . .

—¡Damas y caballeros! ¡Señores y señoras! ¡Estimada concurrencia! ¡Respetable público! ¡Niños de todas edades! ¡abran paso! ¡formen línea! ¡hagan cola! ¡cuidado con los codos! ¡déjenme hablar por favor que voy a empezar! ¡La carpa Peláez! ¡la carpa de toda la familia! ¡La carpa Peláez, la única, la de más prestigio, la de su predilección, se complace en presentarles una función inolvidable! ¡Una función de sana y divertida comedia! ¡no se permiten chistes groseros, hágame el favor! ¡una función de tres horas y media de diversión! ¡oiga usted! ¡tres horas y media! ¡qué me dicen damas y caballeros! ¡tres horas y media de regocijo, de cumplida alegría, de música, de maromas y de balanceo de alambre! ¡Vea las gracias de la divina Tere Peláez en el trapecio de cuarenta pies! ¡veinte metros o más querido público! ¡ver es creer! ¡no empujen que hay asientos para toda la familia! ¡Asómbrese usted! ¡Vengan, vengan y vean y gocen y muéranse de risa con don Chema! don Chon! y ¡don Ciriaco! ¡con doña Lolita! ¡don Cuco! y ¡doña Cuca y Black Espot! su perrito amaestrado, ¡importado desde la capital! ¡El perrito más educado en todo el mundo y en los visibles planetas del universo! ¡oiga usted! ¡No se pierdan la función de esta noche, imponente público de Klail City! ¡Público conocedor y discriminador de esta bella ciudad del Valle! ¡Entren, pasen, vean, gocen, diviértanse aquí con la honesta carpa Peláez! ¡su carpa predilecta, señores y señoras! ¡Un servidor les garantiza tres horas y media de risa y diversión para toda la sagrada familia! ¡Compren sus boletos en la taquilla donde la divina Tere les complacerá atentamente! ¡Pase, gentil público, pase y vaya pasando que se acaban los boletos! . . . ¡Oigan la música, damas y caballeros, novios y novias del lugar! ¡disfruten de ella en sus asientos recién pintados y enumerados por un servidor en su propia mano! ¡No se les olvide, déjenme repetir, no se les olvide! ¡tenemos dulces americanos y nacionales! ¡Caramelos! ¡Cacahuates! ¡tenemos esquite con mantequilla de tres colores en bolsas grandes y en cajas gigantes! ¡no se pierda la aventura! ¡Hay golosinas para todos los gustos! ¡Tenemos charamuscas! ¡tenemos calabazates con almendra! ¡dulces de leche quemada! ¡sodas y leche malteada en cajita de cartón con su propio popote particular para su higiene personal, caro público! ¡dulces de biznaga, pirulís con premios dentro! ¡aquí se vende todo! ¡No se esperen! ¡no malgaste su tiempo! ¡pásele, por aquí, distinguida concurrencia!

—Ya, párale con eso. Esta noche te trepas aquí en la plataforma y das dos o tres saltos mortales mientras Camilo hace la perorata. Tienes talento, chico, y no hay que desperdiciarlo.

—¿Usté cree?

—No lo dudes. Ahora vamos con lo de la carpa otra vez y luego a buscarnos unas botellas vacías para la marimba de Leocadio.

Las botellas vacías se lavaban y luego se les llenaba de agua a un determinado nivel para conseguir de ellas la nota musical adecuada. Leocadio Tovar (en las tablas don Chon) soplaba la trompeta y el trombón, y tocaba la marimba de botellas con más ganas que talento. A veces donde falta una cosa hay que suplirle con otra. Ni modo.

OTRA VEZ LA MUERTE

Había pasado tres años como un día con la Carpa Peláez bajo el ojo paternal de don Víctor. Hombre derecho y recto en su trato y comportamiento, don Víctor, en su aspecto, era alto y flaco aunque gran bebedor de cerveza y, por no despreciar, de lo que la suerte le departiera. Por él me ensené a leer empezando con anuncios de medicinas de patente y de hierbas medicinales; más tarde con periódicos y revistas, hasta llegar a libros de toda especie; en fin, de lo que fuera y como saliera.

Si mis trotes por las calles de Relámpago me habían despabilado, la enseñanza formal, en muy gran parte, pues, se la debía a ese señor. Veterano de la Revolución, don Victor, en un tiempo, también vendió y compró caballos en compañía con su compadre, don Aurelio Alemán, otro coahuilense. Uno de los tratos fue con las fuerzas de don Jesús Carranza, hermano de don Venustiano.

Allá en 1920 estuvo don Víctor como teniente coronel en la zona militar de Papantla, Veracruz. La estancia en las Huastecas potosinas y veracruzanas duro poco más de año; parte de mi lectura provino de unos apuntes que él había hecho durante ese tiempo. Allí aprendí que don Víctor se había casado con Lía Samaniego, hija ella de una de esas viejas familias judías mexicanas. Más tarde, por don Camilo, supe que ella y su hijito, Saúl, y otro, por nacer, murieron a causa de la influenza española que arrambló con familias, pueblos y municipios enteros por los años '19, '20 y '21. Algo parecido a lo que había hecho la viruela unos años antes.

Lo que sigue, pues, forma parte de los escritos de don Víctor. Diré que tengo que aceptar la responsabilidad en el ordenamiento así como en las enmendaciones ortográficas ya que no del contenido, como debe ser.

La parte que aquí incluyo consiste en apuntes hechos en la zona militar de Papantla, Veracruz, y en el Distrito Federal.

143

≫ ≫ ≫

Papantla, Ver., 23 mayo '20

Han asesinado a nuestro paisano, don Venustiano Carranza. Por ahora no se sabe quién lo mandó matar pero como la cosa sucedió en esta zona militar pronto se sabrá. Mi compadre A. ha logrado conseguir 270 caballos; piensa vendérselos a Mirillas. A mí me toca buena parte de ese asunto. Veremos.

Papantla, Ver., 24 mayo '20

Por órdenes del jefe de esta zona militar, el gral. Lázaro Cárdenas, han prendido al gral. Rodolfo Herrero como el presunto asesino de don Venus. Hace rato que me mandó llamar mi gral. Manuel Ávila Camacho dándome así las órdenes para la disposición del reo Herrero. Ahora que M.A.C. ha ascendido a jefe del estado mayor, la zona militar de las Huastecas puede elegir: o se endereza o a ver dónde se mete. Hoy mandé al Indio Vela a que recogiera mis cosas y así estaré listo para cuando tenga que salir para la capital.

Papantla, Ver., 27 mayo '20

. . . nada o poco, que es lo mismo cuando uno está de esperas.

Papantla, Ver., 29 mayo '20

Mañana salgo rumbo a Jalapa para recoger a ocho mochos que me acompañaran como escolta particular a México. Con que sepan su trabajo me conformo. Esta noche me dijo Pepe Figueroa que a don Venus lo mataron a traición. Francamente yo no entiendo por qué se le considera listo a ese abogadillo. Pues, claro, que fue a traición; no me digan que los de Herrero pidieron permiso a la escolta y a Carranza antes de despacharlo. Hay gente en este mundo que . . . Lo de los caballos se está arreglando; ayer mismo se consiguieron treinta y siete más y con eso hace 307, según cuentas.

Jalapa, Ver., 2 junio '20

Vine por ocho y encuentro cinco: dos con licencia de 20 días y el tercero está en el hospital militar. Resulta poco heroica la enfermedad: unas almorranas a causa de comer tunas de nopal.

Papantla, Ver., 4 junio '20

Los cinco que me traje de Jalapa: Evaristo Garrido H., de Tepoztlán, Mor.; Santos Leal Cantú, Cadereyta Jiménez, N.L.; Armando Sánchez Villagómez, Jalostotitlán, Jal.; Jesús Balderas, Atenguillo, Jal.; y Juan de Dios Regüelta, Soliseño, Tamps. Gente decidida.

Con los once de aquí y estos cinco tendré lo suficiente para trasladar a Herrero a México. Esta mañana el Indio Vela me dijo que Herrero estuvo inmiscuido con Guajardo en el asesinato de Zapata el año pasado. Puede ser. El gral. Cárdenas también va a México; comisión delicada. Hay que madrugar; el tren sale a las tres.

México, D.F., 10 junio '20

Esta noche no acompaño a Félix Cáceres. Otra parranda como la del lunes y por poco me quedo tieso. Esta cruda no me la quita ni el Papa. A mí que me den aguardiente de Coahuila o, no habiendo más, el tequila de Jalisco. Lo que es el whiskey americano, nones. Es algo dulzón y luego le cae a uno una cruda como una casa.

Así que acabe con el asunto de Herrero iré a ver a mi mujer y a mi Saúl en Arteaga —y si no, pues, ¿para qué sirve ser uno teniente coronel si no puede largarse de vez en cuando? Veremos.

México, D.F., 18 junio '20

Diez días llevamos aquí; mal negocio. Telegrama de mi compadre A., diciéndome que el asunto caballerizo en rieles, sin complicaciones. Menos mal. Creo que con mi parte voy a comprar aquel terreno cerca de Bella Unión. Tengo 33 años, llevo casi ocho años en la joda y amén de las tres balas que llevo en las piernas, este será el primer jugo que le exprimo a la Bola.

El proceso judicial de Herrero se dio por terminado. Nada. El juez no pudo verificar nada entre lo que dijeron Herrero y Murguía. Me parece raro que don Venus se haya suicidado como dice Herrero; cuatro balazos. Es mucho ese suicidio.

México, D.F., 23 junio '20

Telegrama de mi gral. M.A.C. 15 DIAS LICENCIA STOP VOLVER PAPANTLA 9 JULIO STOP SALUDOS STOP JEFE DEL ESTADO MAYOR, MANUEL AVILA CAMACHO, PAPANTLA, VERACRUZ.

Papantla, Ver., 11 julio '20

Cayó carta de Lía donde me cuenta que el sacerdote insiste en bautizar a Saulito en la iglesia del pueblo. Tendrá que esperarse hasta que llegue yo definitivamente. Yo ni sabía que todavía quedaba iglesia en Arteaga; si mal no recuerdo, los Dávila la quemaron el '13 cuando el supuesto cuartelazo en Saltillo. A uno de esos bandidos lo vi en Culiacán con tamaña lengua de fuera allí donde lo colgó el tuerto Melguizo. El Tuerto Marco Antonio Melguizo . . . Una noche dijo Lucio Blanco que Melguizo vino al mundo a destiempo, antes de que Dios acabara de completarlo: le falta un ojo, tres dedos de una mano y dos de la otra, es cojo de la pierna izquierda y, cuando se precipita, tartamudea. Lo que tiene Melguizo es un par de huevos como martillos de campana y una lealtad a Lucio Blanco que no deja duda de su hombría. ¿Desde cuándo que no veo a esa gente de mi Norte querido?

México, D.F., 14 julio '20

En la capital de nuevo. Antes de salir de la Huasteca me dijo mi gral. Ávila Camacho que me mandaban al estado mayor de Obregón y que de mí dependía lo que hiciera de allí en adelante. Las cartas de recomendación del gral. Cárdenas fueron escritas en su propia mano. Yo no creo que tenga aptitud para el estado mayor pero uno va a donde lo mandan.

El hotelito es modesto y limpio.

México, D.F., 16 julio '20

Me junté con gente del Norte; los más de ellos son de Sonora y Nuevo León y los menos de Tamaulipas. Nosotros, los coahuilenses, parecemos gente extraña, más bien, aparte. Todos congeniamos y uno de Monterrey, Elizondo Carvajal, resultó ser primo hermano de mi compadre Aurelio. Los tres abogados que comieron con nosotros son norteños también; por lo visto tendrían unos doce o catorce años cuando empezó lo de Díaz y Madero. Ahora esa gente es más revolucionaria que la palabra.

México, D.F., 18 julio '20

Grau me mostró la ropa que llevaban don Pancho Madero y Pino Suárez la noche que los mataron. Qué ocurrencias . . . Según Grau encontraron la ropa en los sótanos de la penitenciaria. A Pino Suárez le dieron cinco balazos por la espalda, todos en el lado izquierdo. El grupo de los cinco tiros es bastante reducido; se conoce que los mataron a quemarropa.

Los Huertistas, en su vida, supieron hacer algo bien hecho.

México, D.F., 20 julio '20

Lía no puede venirse a la capital. Dará luz al entrar el año y luego Dios dirá. Mi suegro me mandó un reloj suizo con su leontina de oro. Esta noche los voy a estrenar . . . hace rato vino el Indio Vela para levantarme y se sorprendió al verme escribiendo y listo para salir. Debo estar en la Ciudadela antes de las ocho; lo de Villa quizá no se resuelva ya. Habrá guerra y tiroteo de nuevo. Todavía no puedo entender cómo aguanta tanto el mexicano.

Coincidencia: de repente me acordé de Zapata y en menos de media hora recibí noticias que en Monterrey acababan de fusilar a Guajardo. Pendejearon. Lo debían haber colgado.

≫ ≫ ≫

Según don Camilo, como ya se dijo, su hermano perdió su familia a consecuencias de la influenza española. Pasando unos pocos meses, renunció la carrera militar recibiendo una pensión más bien modesta y se regresó a Arteaga de donde no salió por cinco años. Cuando decidió dejar el exilio impuesto por sí mismo se vino a los Estados Unidos. Llegó, como lo habían hecho tantos antes y, luego, muchos más después, al Valle del Río Bravo.

Don Camilo decía que los años no habían pasado por don Víctor. Cuando me recogió en Relámpago ya llevaba ocho o nueve años rodando por los pueblitos del Valle en la carpa de su hermano.

Tres años como un día.

A don Víctor Peláez le tocó morir en Flora. Después de tantas peripecias, las reumas y unas complicaciones renales lograron matarlo.

Los de la Carpa Habanita y los de la Furriel Hnos. (la de Vicky), asistieron todos. Esta vez sí lloré, como cuando murió mamá. El día siguiente la Carpa Peláez hizo los preparativos para irse rumbo a Ruffing y yo decidí quedarme en Flora; otra vez la muerte, otra vez huérfano y nuevamente al pairo.

FLORA

(y no le busque tres pies al micho) se llama así porque Rufus T. Klail egregio fundador de Klail City, tenía una hija con ese nombre. La gente bien pensada dice que la ciudad tiene el aspecto de la señorita (que no logró casarse): seca, desabrida, llena de malas intenciones y con cara de pocos amigos. Flora está en el condado de Belken y allí, hace muchos años, un tren mató a unas veinte personas que iban en un troque a la yerba. Uno de los sobrevivientes fue Beto Castañeda, muchacho de Klail City que, mucho más tarde, fue yerno del difunto Albino Cordero.

Este relato no es de Beto sino del pueblo de Flora y de lo que allí ocurrió cuando el entierro de Bruno Cano.

Esta gente de Flora es muy alborotadora: tienen concursos de belleza, una cámara de comercio mexicana, organizan bailes al aire libre, juegan al bingo en la iglesia y andan siempre con esto y aquello. No vaya más allá; es gente mitotera.

AI POZO CON BRUNO CANO

¡Cómo que no lo sepulta?

Ya me oyeron.

Sí, le oímos, pero usted tiene que sepultarlo. Si no hay más.

Allá él; yo no lo sepulto. Que lo sepulte otro. . . Ustedes. La iglesia no lo sepultará.

¿La iglesia o usted, don Pedro?

Yo; la iglesia; lo mismo da.

Qué lo mismo ni qué nada: Es usted, ¿qué no?

Sí, yo; pero no me vengan a decir que no tengo razón . . . Miren que echarme de la madre.

Sí, don Pedro, pero si alguien puede perdonar debería ser usted. El cura.

Sí, sí, el cura. Pero también soy hombre.

¿Y quién lo duda? Ándele, sepúltelo y luego nos echamos un trago.

No sé.

Ándele. Anímese, don Pedro. Si usted y don Bruno fueron buenos amigos. Además, la cosa fue de borrachera . . .

No sé.

¿Qué le cuesta? Aquí, Lisandro y yo lo llevamos al cementerio, ¿verdad? ¿Qué tal? ¿Hace? Diga que sí, don Pedro.

Mire, don Pedro, ni a la iglesia lo traemos. De que Salinas lo llevamos derechito al camposanto y allí usted nos lo entierra con sus rezos y todo.

¿Pero de seguro que no lo traen a la iglesia?

Descuide.

Palabra.

Bueno, se lo llevan de que Salinas y dentro de cuarto de hora voy al cementerio. ¿Han visto a Jehú? Lo necesito para el responso.

Ese debe andar por ahí tirando piedras a los pájaros o haciendo un mandado. Déjelo, don Pedro, yo lo hallo.

Ya saben, ni una palabra. Dentro de un cuarto de hora y al pozo
. . . mira, que echarle de la madre a todo un sacerdote de la santa
madre iglesia.

Agradecidos, don Pedro. No se preocupe y gracias, ¿eh? Los
dos hombres se volvieron al centro del pueblo sin cruzar una palabra entre sí ni con la gente que les saludaba. Llegaron a la cantina
de Germán Salinas y anunciaron: Ya se hizo. Hay entierro. Llamen
a los Vega; que traigan la carroza más grande. Cuélenle; avísenle a
todo mundo.

Don Bruno Cano, nativo de Cerralvo, Nuevo León, y vecino de
Flora, Texas, de estado civil viudo y sin progenie ni sucesión,
murió, según el médico, de un ataque al corazón. De un infarto que
lo rindió tan lacio como títere de cuerda. Los que verdaderamente
lo conocían decían que murió de envidia y por andar choteando al
prójimo.

La noche que murió Cano, él y otro compañero, Melitón Burnias, habían acordado a escarbar un lotecito que le pertenecía a
doña Panchita Zuárez, sobandera, partera al pasito y remendona
fina de jovencitas no muy usadas y todavía en servible estado de
merecer. La tía Panchita, según la gente de Flora, tenía un tesoro
escondido en su patio. Esta relación, el nombre dado a los tesoros,
estaba escondida desde los tiempos de Escandón, según unos;
desde los tiempos del general Santa Ana, según otros; y todavía
otros, más cercanos, desde el tiempo de la Revolución . . . tesoro
que fue ocultado por unos ansiosos comerciantes recién emigra-
dos, etc. La cosa es que Bruno Cano y Burnias, entre copa y copa,
acordaron en cavar la tierra, como tantos otros, en busca del tesoro mentado. Melitón Burnias juraba que tenía unos rezos infalibles
para esos asuntos.

Es difícil imaginar dos hombres tan dispares: Cano, gordito,
color de rosa, tacaño certificado, comerciante y dueño del matade-
ro de reces, "La Barca de Oro"; en fin, una de las primeras luces
del pueblo. Burnias, no; Burnias era algo sordo, flaco, chaparrito,
de oficio desconocido y más seco que cagarruta de cabra en agos-

to. También era pobre y de mala suerte. Cuando Tila, la mayor, se largó con Práxedis Cervera, éste volvió con Tila y, juntos, pusieron a Burnias de patitas en la calle. El hombre, dicen, encogió los hombros y se fue a dormir al campo de sandías. Esa misma noche, claro, hubo granizo. Melitón Burnias, sin embargo, no era codicioso y sería por eso, tal vez, que Bruno Cano lo escogió como socio en la búsqueda de la relación. Estaban los dos tomando en que Salinas cuando les sorprendió las once de la noche. Al sonar el reloj cuco los dos se fueron a recoger los talaches, palas y otra herramienta para cavar el lotecito de doña Panchita.

Serían, acaso, como las tres de la mañana y estaban Bruno Cano, dentro del pozo echando tierra arriba, y el sordo de Burnias afuera, desparramándola lo mejor que podía, cuando se oyó un ¡tonc! Bruno escarbó más y otra vez ¡tonc! luego otro, y otro más.

¿Melitón, Melitón, no oíste? Creo que vamos cerca.

¿Qué si no oí? ¿Qué si no oí qué?

Te digo que vamos cerca.

Ah, sí, pues entonces, ¿qué rezo yo?

¿Qué?

¿Que qué rezo yo?

¿Cómo que qué resolló?

¿Qué resolló algo?

¿Qué resolló algo dices?

¿Qué resolló? ¡Ay, Diosito mío!

Diciendo esto, Burnias voló; abandonó la pala y a su socio; empezó a gritar, convencido, tal vez, que un fantasma que resollaba venía por él. Corrió por patios llevándose cercas, resbalando en charcos, atravesando callejones, despertando perros y dando saltos como coneja clueca hasta llegar rendido al campo de sandía donde se echó a rezar en voz alta.

Bruno Cano, entretanto, se había quedado con el aire en la boca. (¿Qué resolló?) (¿Un fantasma?) Así que pudo se puso a gritar y a llorar: ¡Sáquenme! ¡Sáquenme de aquí! ¡Que me matan!

¡Sáquenmeeeeeeeeee! ¡Con una chingada! ¡Ay, yay yay, Diosito santo! ¡Que me saquen! ¡Ayúdenme! ¡Con una chingada! ¡Ay yay yay, Diosito mío! ¡Sáquenme!

En esto, y ya iban para las cinco, don Pedro Zamudio, cura de Flora, iba cruzando el solar de doña Panchita rumbo a la iglesia cuando oyó los alaridos de Bruno. Levantando la sotana para que no se le estropeara tanto, se dirigió al pozo y así, en la oscuridad, le preguntó al que estaba en el pozo:

¿Qué pasa? ¿Qué hace usted allí?

¿Es usted don Pedro? Soy yo, Cano. Sáqueme.

¿Pues qué anda haciendo Ud. por esta vecindad?

Sáqueme primero. Más al luego le cuento.

¿Se golpeó cuando se cayó?

No me caí . . . ayúdeme.

Sí, hijo, sí; ¿pero entonces cómo vino a dar allí? ¿Seguro que no está lastimado?

Segurísimo, señor cura, pero sáqueme ya con una . . . perdón.

¿Qué ibas a decir, hijo?

Nada, padrecito, nada; sáqueme.

No creo que pueda yo sólo; estás algo gordo.

¿Gordo? ¿Gorda su madre!

¿Mi quééééééééé?

Sáqueme ya con una chingada. ¡Ándele!

¡Pues que lo saque su madre!

¡Chingue la suya!

Don Pedro se persignó, se hincó cerca del pozo y se puso a orar aquello de " . . . recoge a este pecador en tu seno" cuando Bruno Cano le mentó de la madre otra vez. Tan clarita fue la mentada que hasta los pájaros dejaron de trinar. Don Pedro, a su vez, sacó el rosario y empezó con la misa de los muertos; esto puso a Cano color de hormiga y estalló con otro chingue a su madre tan redondo y tan sentido como el primero. Estaba para soltar otro cuando don Pedro se levantó extendiendo los brazos en cruz e intonando lo de "tomad a este pecador en tu regazo". Entonces Bruno Cano dejó de hablar y sólo se oían unos soplidos como fuelles. Se acabó el rezo y don Pedro asomó la cabeza al pozo y preguntó: —¿No ve? Con los rezos se allega a la paz. Ya va amaneciendo. Dentro de poco vendrán por usted.

Bruno no le puso cuidado. Ni lo oyó siquiera. Bruno Cano había echado el bofe entre uno de los misterios del rosario y una de las madres. Entregando, así, su alma al Señor, al Diablo o a su madre; a escoger.

Como es de suponer, no menos de treinta personas habían observado la escena. Habíanse quedado a una respetable distancia mientras uno rezaba y el otro maldecía.

Pero, como quiera que sea, lo sepultaron y en campo sagrado. Para el pesar de don Pedro Zamudio, el entierro estuvo muy concurrido. La cosa duró cerca de siete horas. Hubo doce oradores, cuatro coros, (uno de varoncitos y uno de chicas, otro de mujeres de la Vela Perpetua y el cuarto de hombres del Sagrado Corazón de Jesús; todos de blanco). Los Vega trajeron el cuerpo de Bruno en la carroza morada con la cortinita gris a fleco. Además de don Pedro, fuimos los doce monaguillos cada uno vestido en casulla negra y blanca bien almidonada. La gente de los otros pueblos del Valle pronto se dio cuenta que algo había en Flora y se dejó venir en troque, en rides, en bicicleta y unos de Klail hasta alquilaron un Greyhound que ya venía repleto de gente procedente de Bascom.

Aparecieron tres dulceros y empezaron a vender raspas para combatir aquel sol que derretía las calles de chapapote. La concurrencia, y yéndose por lo bajo, no era menos de cuatro mil almas. Unos, de seguro, ni sabían a quién enterraban; los más ni conocieron a Cano; lo que pasa es que a la gente le gusta la bulla y no pierde ripio para salir de casa.

Don Pedro tuvo que aguantarse y rezó no menos de trescientos Padrenuestros entre Aves y Salves. Cuando se puso a llorar (de coraje, de histeria, de hambre, vaya usted a saber) la gente, compadecida, rezó por don Pedro. Los oradores repitieron las elegías varias veces y los de la raspa, cada uno, tuvieron que comprar otras tres barras de hielo de cien libras para dar abasto a toda la gente. En casos ni sirope echaban ya. La gente se comía el hielo con o sin agua. De su parte, los coros pronto disiparon su repertorio; para no desperdiciar la oportunidad, se echaron el *Tantum Ergo* que no venía al caso y, menos, el "Ven, Buen Pastor, Redentor Celestial" que se oía sólo en Pascuas. Por fin los cuatro coros se juntaron y entonces la cosa se puso más fina.

A pesar del calorón, el polvo, el empujar y la multitud agolpada y remolinándose, no hubo mayor desorden: un pleito que otro, sí, pero sin navajas. Lo que sí se contó fueron los que cayeron: hubo no menos de treinta y cuatro desmayados y fue, en fin, un entierro como Dios manda.

El que no asistió fue Melitón Burnias. Como decía después, "Ese día yo andaba ocupadísimo".

La gente casi ni le ponía atención.

DON JAVIER

Trece años de tener a Gela de querida y ahora me sale que ella y su hermana se van, que piensan abrir una tienda y vender ropa a la gente de los ranchos. Así que vuelva Jehú con la contestación le doy otra carta y a ver qué pasa.

Pinche suerte; no poder ir a verla porque hoy se le ocurre a Angelita celebrar nuestras bodas de plata. ¡Qué ocurrencias! Esto le pasa a uno por ser blando de corazón.

(La Gela es un fierro; una res de calidad; una fiera en la cama; un cuero como pocos; una de las pocas que quedan.)

No tiene ni qué; la culpa de todo la tiene la hermana, vieja flaca, tísica y espantapájaros.

¿Dónde chingaos se habrá metido ese cabrón de Jehú?

EMILIO TAMEZ

A Emilio Tamez le falta la oreja derecha. No nació así, se la cortó el menor de los Murillo en la cantina de don Florentino.

¿Como una rebanada de pan?

Así; igualito.

Emilio Tamez cojea, resultado de un accidente cuando tendría unos once años. El Emilio andaba saltando de vagón en vagón cuando se resbaló en un pedazo de bróculi y ¡zas! al suelo, cabrón. A pesar de las sobadas y el aceite volcánico, la pierna izquierda le quedó más corta que la otra.

Ahora, para compensar, cojea de la pierna izquierda y no oye por el oído derecho. Emilio sabe leer y escribir en inglés y español; con todo eso, no se le quita lo pendejo.

¡Hazte un lado, chueco, jijo-de-la-chingada!

LA TÍA PANCHITA

¿Dónde está el enfermo?

Aquí, tía Panchita; pásele.

Oh, pos si es Rafa . . . ¿qué te pasa, criatura?

No sabemos; ayer empezó a tartamudear y ahora ahí esta titereteando con calentura.

Bueno; corran las Cortinas, sálganse todos y cierren la puerta que voy a empezar.

La tía Panchita extrajo un huevo pardo de la bolsa de provisión y lo cruzó por la cara de Rafa Buenrostro. Después hizo otra señal de la cruz cubriendo el cuerpo entero del enfermo y empezó su rezo:

Oración y ensalmo para susto: Criatura de Dios, yo te curo y te ensalmo en el nombre de Dios y el Espíritu Santo. Tres personas distintas y un sólo Dios verdadero. San Roque, San Sebastián, once mil vírgenes por tu Glorísima Pasión y Ascensión dígnense a curar a esta afligida criatura de ojo, espanto, calentura o cualquier otra curación no refiriendo a tan linda persona que se refiere a su sacrosanto misterio. Jesús criatura de Dios acuérdate de tu Dios. Cuánto amante está Jesús, cuánto amante está Jesús, así sea. Amén.

Ofrecimiento. Jesús sea tu doctor, María Santísima tu doctora y que esta enfermedad sea aventada por el amor de Dios, por el amor de Dios, amén.

❧ ❧ ❧

La tía Panchita repitió la oración, el ensalmo y el ofrecimiento dos veces más y entonces estrelló el huevo en un plato verde que colocó debajo de la cama. Rafa Buenrostro respiro hondamente y empezó un sueño que duraría día y medio.

La tía Panchita se despidió apresuradamente diciendo que volvería el miércoles. Mujer ocupadísima, la tía se dirigía al bautizo del niño de Lino Carrizales.

EPIGMENIO SALAZAR

Este tiene una casa con cuartos para alquilar y es el propietario de una hernia que le ha permitido estar de huevón desde antes de la guerra mundial número dos.

Epigmenio ve muchas cosas y lo que no ve lo suple con su imaginación. Así, como dice, nunca está en servicio inactivo. Por ejemplo, él sabe lo que hay entre don Javier y la Gela; conoce de buena tinta lo que hay entre el cocinero de El Fénix y la chica de la farmacia; sabe, por vías fidedignas, lo que le pasa a la esposa del menor de los Murillo.

Lo que ignora Epigmenio es por qué se enganchó esa hernia como una casa.

LA GÜERA FIRA

Sin rodeos: la güera Fira es puta. No la hace de puta (como las criadas) ni putea (como las amas de las criadas); no. La güera Fira es puta y ya. Hay más. La güera Fira tiene los ojos azules, el pelo corto y no tiene que pintárselo y tiene unas formas que le quitarían el hipo al cura don Pedro Zamudio.

La güera Fira no es de aquí, que es de Jonesville-on-the-River. Hija de mujer mexicana de Jonesville y de un soldado bolillo de Fort Jones: no fue la primera que saliera ni la última, pero, la verdad, seguramente tiene que ser la mujer más hermosa del Valle. (El que sí sabe mucho más de la gente de Jonesville-on-the-River es don Américo Paredes.)

La güera Fira es una mujer seria que lleva su putería como las chicas de la escuela llevan los libros: con naturalidad. Al bañarse, huele a agua y jabón y cuando sale a la calle rumbo a su trabajo, todavía le quedan húmedos los ricitos en la sien.

Trabaja en la cantina de Félix Champión, un hijo ilegítimo de mi tío Andrés, y no baila ni anda de mesa en mesa ni coquetea ni hace papeles. Don Quixote contaba que eso de ser alcahuete era cosa seria; puede ser, pero el oficio de puta en cantina pobre de pueblo ruin tampoco es para morirse de risa.

Las mujeres de Klail saben quién es y qué es y ya. Si murmuran, allá ellas pero las más no, las más no murmuran. Las mujeres suelen ser comprensivas cuando les da la gana.

Lo malo es que la güera Fira no durará mucho en Klail: es demasiado pequeño y, la verdad, el dinero escasea.

ARTURO LEYVA

Cuando Arturo se casó con Yolanda Salazar, hija de don Epigmenio (el que no trabaja), ya chambeaba con los Torres, los de la tienda de ladrillo. Arturo es tenedor de libros y para engraciarse con su suegro le lleva los libros gratis y, no pendejo, procura ordeñar parte de la renta para que don Epigmenio tenga dinero que gastar de vez en cuando. Todo esto, se entiende, sin que lo sepa doña Candelaria Munguía de Salazar, esposa y cruz particular del Caballero de la Hernia.

A Candelaria le duran las criadas algo así como la viruela loca, cosa de dos semanas. Una vez contrató a Tere Malacara, q.e.p.d., pero Tere sólo duró dos días: uno con don Epigmenio y el segundo con Arturo. La Tere era pobre, maltrechita pero honrada; cosas todas que, a veces, acuerdan en una persona.

Estaría de más decir que Tere mandó a los Salazar con viento nuevo.

DON MANUEL GUZMÁN

Ex lechero, ex dueño de tres sastrerías, ex socio de una panadería y ex policía del barrio mexicano de Klail City. Esa fue una vida de don Manuel.

Aquí va otra. Peón, domador de caballos, ex revolucionario, siguió esa huella tan conocida: Villa, Obregón, decepción.

Nacido en Campacuás, condado de Hidalgo, estado de Texas, jugaba al monte de tres barajas y con albur. Sabía marcar cartas y lo hacía usando un alfiler o una aguja con color rojo tenue que sólo él podía ver.

Cómo llegó a ser policía en el barrio mexicano de Klail no podré decirles.

En otras vidas trabajó en el arroz, fue jornalero en el ferrocarril y —una temporada— estuvo de pastor en Wyoming. Hombre andariego, don Manuel se casó con una mujer fuerte y comprensiva que conoció bastante bien a su hombre para no molestarlo con esas menudencias que la iglesia y la sociedad (esas hermanas chismosas) imponen para hacerle la vida pesada al prójimo.

Don Manuel no tomaba ni fumaba pero era muy maldiciente, corajudo, mal sufrido y corto de paciencia. Gran contador de cuentos que no de chistes, nunca oí que se la recargara. Si llegaba a cansar a la gente sería cuando se ponía a alabar a sus cinco hijos. No contando el menor, vio a todos casarse y hasta llegó a conocer a varios de sus nietos.

Como ocurre a veces con esa gente que vive varias vidas y entre ellas unas agitadas, don Manuel vino a morirse de un derrame cerebral cuando hablaba con su mujer mientras ella le quitaba los botines.

EL MAISTRO

A Lucas Barrón, el dueño de la cantina Aquí Me Quedo, le dicen el Chorreao.

¿Porque nunca se baña?

Exacto.

El Chorreao tiene muchos clientes y, entre ellos, uno muy especial: El Maistro, don Genaro Castañeda. El Maistro es pintor de casas y una vez, hace muchos años, el gobierno lo llamó a las armas: que prestara sus servicios para la defensa de la nación contra sus enemigos y en pro de la libertad, etc., etc.

Era la primera guerra mundial y al Maistro se lo llevaron. Primero a San Antonio para el examen físico (donde te meten el dedo cordial en el culo para ver si tienes almorranas), luego a otro campamento militar que nunca logró averiguar dónde estaba. Al fin llegaron al puerto de New York, diría yo, y a cruzar esos mares hasta Francia donde se guerreaba entonces.

Según El Maistro no la pasó tan mal. Hablaba un poco de inglés, comía lo que había y le pagaban casi cada mes aunque no sabía dónde gastarlo. Recuerda que una vez, estando en la trinchera, le pegó un pedazo de metal del tamaño de posta, así como las bi-bis. Al sentir el golpecito se llevó la mano a la frente y vio la bolita. Dice que se le quedó viendo un rato y como no le pasó nada, pues, la dejó caer al charco de agua donde estaba de guardia.

Se sacó un rasguño bastante largo a causa de los alambres de púa y así fue cómo derramó unas gotas de sangre en suelo francés. Cuando se paró el cañoneo lo pusieron en otro barco, cruzó el mar, luego, por tren, lo llevaron de nuevo a San Antonio. Allí le dieron más dinero y lo despacharon en bus para Klail de donde no ha vuelto a salir.

El Maistro, andando el tiempo, se casó y junto con su mujer tuvieron un bolón de hijos. Como dice él, unos vivos y otros brutos pero todos comen.

Hombre pacífico, El Maistro, como muchos pintores, es gran bebedor de cerveza, whiskey, vino y lo que aparezca. Será un azar de la profesión —¿quién sabrá? pero así es y en paz. El Maistro tendrá sus 75 años pero todavía pinta y, la verdad, todavía se echa un trago o dos o lo que tolere el hígado. Con sus dos amigos, Echevarría y Leal, que son más o menos de la misma camada, El Maistro se pone a conversar de esas cosas propias de los viejitos de Klail y de todo el mundo.

Supe por casualidad que era veterano de la primera guerra y no le molesto con preguntas aunque me gusta su conversación. Yo estuve en lo de Corea un buen rato y aunque joven y todo, parece que al Maistro y a mí nos pasó casi lo mismo: la experiencia pasó como las nubes que se desbaratan con aire y tiempo.

El American Legion Post en Klail es nuevo, desde la guerra mundial número dos y el nombre en la puerta es el de Pfc. Joseph T. Hargan que murió en el '43 cuando lo de Salerno. Los de la cámara de comercio, los interesados y los ansiosos, esos del Rotary y Leones, no sabían que El Maistro era veterano de la primera guerra. Quizá no les importe . . .

Ahí viene El Maistro.

¿Qué se le ofrece, don Genaro?

Aquí, Rafa; una Perla para mí y otra para Echevarría y una Yax para Leal.

Descuide, don Genaro, yo se las llevó al booth.

Gracias, hijo.

El Maistro vuelve a su mesa donde le esperan sus dos amigos y yo les escojo las cervezas más frías.

VOCES DEL BARRIO

Cuando el sol se baja y los bolillos dejan sus tiendas, el pueblo americano se duerme para no despertar hasta el día siguiente.

Cuando el sol se baja y la gente ha cenado, el pueblo mexicano se aviva y se oyen las voces del barrio: la gente mayor, los jóvenes, los chicos, los perros . . .

Dicen que la Sooner Contracting de Ardmore anda buscando gente . . .

Si no me equivoco, uno de los contratistas es Víctor Jara, "El Pirulí".

¿Con ese? Ni a cruzar la calle, contimás el estado.

Niños, váyanse a jugar a la calle y dejen a los mayores hablar.

¡A la momita, a la momita! Ese poste de telefón es el home-base.

Tules virules, nalgas azules.

Juan Barragán bebe leche y caga pan.

¡No se vale ver, no se vale ver!

Te las hago largas a ti y a Vargas, sino las das, ¿pa qué las cargas?

Pin marín de don pingüé

Cúcara, mácara, pípere fue

Dos y dos son cuatro; cuatro y dos son seis; seis y dos son ocho: y ocho, diez y seis.

Cuenta la tablita
que ya la conté
Cuéntala de vuelta
que ya me cansé.

¿Y por qué no saliste anoche?

No me dejaron; ya sabes. ¿Te quedaste esperando?

Hasta la una.

Pobrecito.

No te burles.

165

Si no me burlo, Jehú . . . ándale, vámonos al parque.

¿Y tu hermanito?

Ahí anda, jugando a las escondederas.

Vente.

Cuidado que nos ven agarrados de la mano.

Ah, raza . . .

¿De veras te quedaste esperando?

Hasta la una . . .

¿Y qué le dijo la enfermera, doña Faustina?

Pues casi nada, quiere que le saquemos las anginas al niño.

¿Y eso pa qué?

Dice que sin anginas no le darán tantos catarros.

Esas son cosas de los gringos que no tienen más que hacer.

Ahora voy yo, ahora voy yo: ¿Quieren tortillas duras?

¡No!

¿Duras?

¡No!

Ah, ¡durazno!

Ahora yo, que va la mía: Lana sube, lana baja.

¡La navaja!

No sé, cuñao, eso de irse con contratista desconocido está arriesgado.

De acuerdo, si hay veces que con los conocidos . . .

Claro . . . Verdá . . . Ya lo creo . . .

¡No me explico, Federico?

¡Me entiendes, Méndez?

No me chingues, Juan Domínguez.

¡Niños, no molesten a los mayores!

Creo que ya es hora de irnos. ¿Dónde estará Adela? Eh, tú, Andrés ¿qué se hizo tu hermana?

La dejé en el parque, amá.

Ve por ella, ándale. Hasta mañana, doña Faustina.

Si Dios es servido, doña Barbarita.

Ahora le toca al barrio dormir. En los barrios se habla de mucho y, como de milagro, siempre se halla de qué hablar noche tras noche.

El barrio puede llamarse el Rebaje, el de las Conchas, el Cantarranas, el Rincón del Diablo, el Pueblo Mexicano —verdaderamente los títulos importan poco.

Lo importante, como siempre, es la gente.

¿Quién es ese muchacho, Genaro?

Se llama Rafa Buenrostro.

¿De cuáles Buenrostro?

¿De los de Julián?

No, éste es de Jesús Buenrostro al que llamaban don Jesús.

Ah, sí; murió joven.

¿Ese fue el que trabajó con el viejo Burns?

No. Ese fue Julián. Don Jesús tenía unas tierras cerca del Carmen.

¿Dónde se echaron a los rinches?

Ahí mero.

Ya, ya. A don Jesús le decían El Quieto.

¿El quieto?

Sí; újule Leal tú ya no te acuerdas de nada.

¿Y quién es el otro?

¿El que se acaba de ir?

No, el que acaba de llegar.

Ah, ése es Jehú Malacara.

¿De los Malacara de Relámpago?

Esos meros. Este es de Roque el que se casó con Tere.

¿La de las maromas?

No, hombre. La de las maromas era Peláez, hija de don Camilo y doña Chucha. La madre de este muchacho era hija de don Jehú Vilches.

El yerno de don Braulio Tapia.

Ándale . . . Ya caigo.

¿Tú conociste a don Braulio, Echevarría?

Cómo no, aunque yo era mucho más chico.

Este muchacho trabajó con los Peláez en las maromas y lo medio crió don Víctor.

Buena persona, don Víctor.

Ya lo creo. ¿Nos echamos otra, muchachos?

Oye, ¿cuántas llevamos ya?

¿Dos, tú?

No sé. ¿Serán tres?

Miren, acaba de llegar don Manuel.

Don Manuel ve a los ancianos y se sienta con ellos mientras espera que Rafa Buenrostro le traiga su café negro.

¿En qué estaban?

En lo mismo, ya sabe. Nos estamos acabando los viejos, don Manuel.

Quite usted, don Genaro. Nosotros cuatro tenemos bastante parque y munición todavía.

Dios lo oiga, don Manuel.

Así sea.

Muchacho, bájale a esa música que los vecinos se quejan del ruido.

Sí, don Manuel.

Voy a estar en la esquina, cuando quieran un aventón me avisan.

Los tres viejitos le dan las gracias, como siempre, y don Manuel Guzmán se sale a andar por esas calles de Klail City, uno de tantos pueblos en el condado de Belken en el Valle del Río Grande de Texas.

Por esas cosas que pasan

EXTRACTO DEL *The Klail City Enterprise-News*
(March 15, 1970)

Klail City. (Special) Baldemar Cordero, 30, of 169 South Hidalgo Street, is in the city jail following a row in a bar in the city's Southside. Cordero is alleged to have fatally stabbed Arnesto Tamez, also 30, over the affections of one of the "hostesses" who works there.

No bail had been set at press time.

POR ESAS COSAS QUE PASAN*

No hay que darle vueltas. Yo maté al Ernesto Tamez en la cantina Aquí Me Quedo. No me pida detalles porque ni yo mismo sé cómo fue. Pero no tiene vuelta de hoja el tal Ernesto; lo dejé tieso.

Lo que son las cosas, ¿eh? Ayer mismo estaba yo pisteando con mi cuñado, Beto Castañeda, el que se casó con mi hermana Marta, y estábamos zonceando y riéndonos de una ocurrencia sobre no sé qué cuando entró Tamez echando madres a manga tendida. A mí me la rayó así, a boca de jarro, pero se la dejé pasar aunque ni nos llevábamos él y yo.

Usted conoció a Tamez, ¿verdad? Una vez en que Félix Champión alguien le atizó semejante botellazo en la nuca después que Tamez rompió el espejo aquel, ¿recuerda? Bueno, a mí no se me ha olvidado y por eso cuando veía a Tamez, pues, si no le sacaba la vuelta, por lo menos tampoco lo perdía de vista.

Así, como le dije, estábamos Beto y yo frotándonos unas cervezas hasta que, como casi siempre sucedía, se nos acababa el conqué o nos poníamos cuetes pero sin molestar a nadie pidiendo cerveza de gorra, ni nada.

Yo a Tamez y a toda su ralea los conocía desde la escuela y cuando vivían en el Rebaje: Joaquín, el mayor, se casó con Jovita de Anda que aunque antes era más puta que las gallinas, parece que se arregló cuando se casó con Joaquín. Emilio, el chueco, quedó así cuando se resbaló de un tren de carga en la plataforma de Chico Fernández. La tal Bertita se casó con uno de los Leal que salió muy jalador y se fue, dicen, a Muleshoe. También dicen que está muy rico y ojalá que así sea porque taloneaba como pocos y merecido se lo tiene. La Bertita no era lo que se dice una ganga

---

*Nota del editor: La grabación en cinta magnetofónica que hizo Balde Cordero fue enmendada sólo en lo que va de ortografía. Ciertamente, lo que importa aquí es el contenido no la forma. Marzo 16, 1970. Klail City Workhouse.

pero tampoco era una mujer mala. El Ernesto era otra cosa. Todavía no puedo comprender cómo se salvó de tantas paradas que me hizo hasta que lo calé yo en el Aquí Me Quedo. En fin . . .

Aquí no se le miente a nadie. Usted me conoce, Hinojosa, igual que conoció a mis padres. Empezamos el pedo Beto y yo en el San Diego, lo seguimos en el Diamond y, todavía a pie, nos llegamos al Blue Bar hasta que llegaron los Reyna. De estos, ni hablar, porque hasta las piedras saben que cuando andan motos se zambullen una cerveza para que la chota crea que andan pistos y no con la Juana encima. Al llegar los Reyna nos fuimos nosotros para que no hubiera mitote. Anselmo Reyna, desde que le di aquella chinga de perro bailarín en el Diamond, me trata con mucha consideración. Pero, al verlos motos y para no alborotar, decidimos irnos al Aquí Me Quedo.

Curioso ¿eh? que si los Reyna no hubieran ido al Blue Bar no hubiera pasado nada. Puro pedo. Cuando algo va a suceder, sucede; ¿para qué irse contra viento y marea? Al Ernesto ya le tocaba anoche y yo tenía que ser el que lo iba a despachar. Algo así como despacha una orden de mercancía el Luisito Moncivάis, ese joto que lleva los libros en que los Torres. A veces me da miedo pensar que maté a un cristiano. ¡Qué cosas! ¿Verdad?

Fíjese, Hinojosa, me acuerdo del por qué pero no del cuándo. Que a mí me la mienten en general qué más da . . . pero que se le enfrenten a uno, así, de sopetón, luego, agréguele usted que andaba yo medio jalao y que Ernesto era un hinchapelotas que me debía unas cuantas paradas de ésas y, para acabarla, que era un bato furris que me caía peseta por lo fanfarrón . . . pues, ¿qué quiere? Nos agarramos.

Beto me dijo después que a él le chisporroteó sangre en el brazo y en la cara. Beto también dijo que yo ni pestañeé ni nada. De mi parte le diré que no oí nada: ni los gritos de las viejas, ni el remolino de los mirones que se acercaron. Nada.

Me acuerdo que salí a la banqueta y que vi una casa donde estaba una familia viendo televisión. Tan inocentes de lo que acababa de suceder como yo lo había estado hacía unos cinco minutos. Dejando de chingaderas, eso de la vida y la muerte infunde cierto miedo porque uno, verdaderamente, no sabe nada de nada.

¿No le dije que una vez el Ernesto, en frente de todos, me quitó una vieja en El Farol? Sí, como lo oye. En otra ocasión le dijo a otra que yo tenía una purgación. Me hizo tantas otras chingaderas parecidas pero por esas cosas que pasan, no le hice nada. Mejor le hubiera cortado el pedo allí . . . pero ¡vaya usted a saber! A lo mejor, no, ¿verdad?

Bueno, anoche no sólo me la rayó en la cara sino que también se rió de mí y me dijo que me faltaban huevos y pelos en el pecho. Eso a mí no me lo dice nadie a no ser que me lleve con él, como usted sabe. Yo no le dije nada, nomás me le quedé viendo y el pendejo tal vez se creyó que le tenía miedo. Siguió jodiendo y se trajo a una de las viejas que bailan en el Aquí Me Quedo y me echó en cara que me había rajado otras veces. Creo que la vieja estaba entre asustada y avergonzada pero, no pendeja, ni chistó. Recuerdo, casi, que me empezaron a zumbar los oídos como si en vez de sombrero llevara encima un panal de avispas. Seguía el zumbido, oía la voz cargante de aquel menso, veía la sonrisa idiotizada de la vieja, y, de repente, oí un grito desgarrador y vi que Ernesto se deslizaba de los brazos de la vieja.

Sí recuerdo que respiré hondamente y que salí del lugar a la banqueta donde divise una familia reunida en la sala viendo la televisión. Más tarde me di cuenta que en la mano zurda llevaba la navaja de cachas blancas que me había regalado papá Albino.

Entré de nuevo a la cantina y de nuevo salí. Ni traté de correr. ¿Para qué? Y, ¿adónde me iba si todos me conocían? Cuando entré otra vez vi que habían echado agua al piso de cemento y que habían barrido la sangre como si tal cosa. Al Ernesto se lo llevaron a la bodega donde tienen la cerveza y la carne seca para la botana. Cuando llegó don Manuel yo mismo le entregué la navaja y me fui con él en su carro cuando acabó lo que tenía que hacer. Después, al bote, ya ve.

Muy de mañana me trajo café uno de los hijos de don Manuel y se esperó hasta que me lo tomara. Fíjese que he tratado de acordarme del momento preciso cuando sepulté la navaja en el pecho de aquel baboso y nada. En blanco. También puede ser que no quiera acordarme . . .

Beto se acaba de ir diciendo que tiene que ir al district attorney para una declaración. Más tarde, quién dirá, pero por ahora me siento mal por lo que hice anoche . . . Eso de que a lo hecho, pecho, son puras ganas de hablar. Créame, me molesta que haya tenido que matar al Ernesto Tamez. A veces pienso que eso de quitarle la vida al prójimo está de la patada.

Hice mal, lo reconozco, pero a veces también pienso que si Ernesto me insultara de nuevo, pues de nuevo lo mataría. La verdad, uno nunca aprende.

No le canso más que veo que me repito por ser esto lo único que me interesa. Gracias por la venida y ya sabe que se agradecen los cigarros. Tal vez algún día yo mismo sepa verdaderamente por qué lo maté —pero ¡qué quiere! él se iba a morir un día de estos y ya estaría que yo le adelantara la fecha. Fíjese, ya estoy de nuevo.

Ah; antes de que se vaya: dígale a Mr. Royce que mañana no estaré en el jale. Ni modo. Mire, también dígale que me debe una semana de raya . . .

Hasta luego, Hinojosa . . . y gracias, ¿eh?

MARTA CUENTA LO SUYO*

. . . no, pos, sabe que cuando murió papá Albino como resultado de aquel accidente en Saginaw, Balde decidió que nos quedáramos allí hasta que se resolviera el asunto. De primero, el contratista que nos trajo desde el Valle, se portó muy mal y Balde tuvo que amenazarlo para que hiciera algo. Con lo poco que le sacamos, Balde contrató a un abogado para la demanda a la Dailey Pickle. El abogado ese era jovencito pero ladino porque hizo que la mentada compañía pepinera nos pagara algo que llaman indemnización. Cuando se resolvió lo de papá, pagamos lo que debíamos de una vez y hasta nos sobró lo suficiente para pasar el tiempo de frío mientras nos enganchábamos con otro contratista o hallábamos trabajo. (Para este tiempo, Beto ya andaba haciéndome la ronda pero por lo del luto, usted comprenderá, no tenía entrada en la casa.)

Usted conoce a Balde desde niño y, como decía papá, qué quiere que le diga. Mamá lleva muchos años de estar tullida y así con sus achaques y todo no ha dejado de hacer los viajes con nosotros. Bien, allí estábamos varias familias mexicanas en Saginaw, aguardando el frío y con el intento de trabajar en lo que saliera. El primero que consiguió trabajo fue Balde como watchimán en el puerto; poco después, le consiguió un puesto allí a Beto, así es que los dos se hicieron más amigos y luego, como usted ya sabe, se hicieron cuñados cuando Beto y yo nos casamos. En ese entonces Balde tenía 27 años y muchas oportunidades de casarse pero, parte por lo de mamá y parte por la necesidad en casa, pues nunca se casó. Cuando volvimos al Valle hace dos años, siguió en las mismas. Balde es noble y trabajador, es más, cuando salía de casa a cervecear, se apartaba de pleitos lo más que podía para no faltar en casa. (Le han sucedido casos en que ha tragado mucha hiel pero se ve que piensa en nosotras y por eso trata de evitar zafarranchos y alboro-

---

*Grabado el 17 de marzo de 1970.

tes.) Yo casi lo único que sé de esto es por lo que Beto me cuenta, pero son contadas las veces que habla de sus asuntos. Una vez, por casualidad, oí que Balde le había dado una santa golpiza a uno de los Reyna pero de eso no se habló en casa.

Mire que es difícil de contarle a usted lo que pensé o lo que dije cuando ocurrió lo de Neto Tamez. De primero no podía o no quería creerlo, tal vez no podía imaginármelo, sabe, porque no me cabía en la cabeza que mi hermano Balde matara a alguien. No crea que lo digo porque Balde sea un santo, no, pero seguramente debía ser algo grueso que Balde no pudo remediar. Le diré que le había costado mucho trabajo dominarse a sí mismo y puede ser que esa noche el tal Ernesto se sobrepasó: Beto me había contado de ciertas paradas hechas por el Neto Tamez pero como Beto habla tan poco no siempre logro entender todo lo que dice. Por parte de Balde, nada, o punto menos, porque lo único que de la calle traía a casa era una sonrisa en la boca. Eso sí, de vez en cuando lo veía más serio que en velorio pero, quite usted, qué le iba a preguntar yo nada. Pues, ya ve, con esos dos hombres, la casa, la comida y la lavada, y con mamá como está, bastante tengo yo pa andar en chismes.

No me hago la inocente, no, sólo que quiero decirle que mucho de lo que sé lo oí de Beto, o de las amigas que venían a vernos o, en las raras veces que Balde y Beto discutían. Lo que me suponía también se lo estoy diciendo, pero ya le advertí que una no sabe todo, ni mucho menos. Todo mundo sabe que Neto Tamez siempre andaba de picabuches con mi hermano Balde y que mi hermano se las dejaba pasar. Yo le digo a usted que si Balde no le paró bola a Neto antes fue porque pensaba en nosotras. Esa es la verdad. Lo que no sabe la gente es por qué Neto se portaba así con mi hermano.

Le voy a contar: desde la escuela el tal Neto me mandaba cartas, me seguía a la casa y usaba a los que le tenían miedo como mensajeros. Yo nunca le puse cuidado ni le di esperanzas tampoco. Las muchachas me contaban que no dejaba que otros muchachos se me acercaran como si él fuera el que mandaba en mí o tal cosa. De esto hace años, y no le dije nada a Balde, pero la primera vez que oí que Neto le haría la vida pesada yo sabía o creía saber por qué lo haría. No sé si Balde sabía o no pero, como dice Beto, todo puede ser.

Una vez mis amigas me contaron que en esos lugares como La Golondrina y El Farolito, Neto Tamez insultó a Balde varias veces y de varias maneras; ya le quitaba la bailadora, o hablaba mal de Balde o hacía cualquier otra perrería, pero siempre con el mismo propósito: el de hacerle la vida pesada, ¿no ve? No digo que Tamez lo seguía no, pero le estoy diciendo que tampoco perdía la oportunidad de estarlo machacando hasta que Balde se iba del lugar. Conste que vivir en el mismo pueblo, casi en el mismo barrio, y soportarle tantas barrabasadas es cosa de mucha paciencia. Balde no hacía corajes en casa y cuando volvía tornado o sano, era el mismo: un beso a mamá, platicaba un rato con nosotras y después se sentaba a fumar en el corredor. Comparado a Balde, Beto, que no habla mucho, parece una chachalaca.

Los Tamez son bastante raros. Cuando vivían en el Rebaje, parece que esa gente andaba de pleitos con los vecinos y con medio mundo. Me acuerdo que cuando el Joaquín, por esas cosas que pasan, se tuvo que casar con Jovita de Anda, don Servando Tamez no permitió que ninguno de los de Anda fuera al casamiento. Cuentan que el pobre de don Marcial de Anda, un hombrecito que no servía para nada, lloró como un niño. Me acuerdo ver al Emilio con su pata corta paseándose en frente de la casa como si fuera policía. Menos mal que la pobre doña Tula Tamez ya había muerto para ese tiempo. Posiblemente lo único bueno que haya salido de esa casa fue Bertita, la que quiso ser novia de Balde. Por fin se huyó con Ramiro Leal, el de la tortillería . . .

Bueno, de todas maneras, ayer, así que usted fue a ver a Balde a la cárcel, llegó don Manuel Guzmán. Dijo que vino a saludar a mamá pero de verás vino a decirle que no se preocupara ella por los gastos de la casa. (¡Quién lo diría! A ese hombre yo le he visto derramar trompadas, cañonazos, patadas y maldiciones a más de cien borrachos y marihuanos para luego llevarles café a la cárcel el día siguiente. Eso sí, desde que don Manuel está de policía, una mujer puede andar sola y de noche por esas calles, y ni quién la moleste.) Al salir, don Manuel me dijo que podíamos sacar la provisión en que los Torres.

Mamá y yo estamos solas sin Balde pero gracias a Dios que todavía tengo a Beto. Ojalá que los Tamez no vengan a buscarle bulla a él porque entonces sí nos hundimos mamá y yo sin un hombre en casa. Beto horita anda en la oficina del district attorney donde está haciendo una declaración como testigo.

Ay, Sr. Hinojosa, no sé dónde vaya a parar lo nuestro . . . En fin, Dios dirá.

ROMEO HINOJOSA
Attorney at Law

4420 South Cerralvo   Tel. 843-1640

Lo que sigue es la declaración en inglés que hizo Beto Castañeda, hoy, el 17 de marzo de 1970, en el despacho del señor Robert
A. Chapman, asistente del procurador por el condado de Belken.

El susodicho oficial de la corte me concedió la declaración
como parte del testimonio en el juicio *The State v. Cordero*, que se
asignó para el 23 de agosto del mismo año en la corte del juez
Harrison Phelps que preside sobre la corte del distrito estatal
número 139.

Romeo Hinojosa
_____
Romeo Hinojosa

A DEPOSITION FREELY GIVEN

on this seventeenth day of March 1970, by Mr. Gilberto Castañeda in room 218 of the Belken County Court House was duly taken,
witnessed and signed by Miss Helen Chacón, a legal interpreter
and acting assistant deputy recorder for said County, as part of a
criminal investigation assigned to Robert A. Chapman, assistant
district attorney for the same County.

It is understood that Mr. Castañeda is acting solely as a deponent and is not a party to any civil or criminal investigation, pro-
ceeding or violation which may be alluded to in this deposition.

"Well, my name is Gilberto Castañeda, and I live
at 169 South Hidalgo Street here in Klail. It is
not my house; it belong to my mother-in-law, but I
have live there since I marry Marta (Marta Cordero
Castañeda, 169 South Hidalgo Street, Klail City)
about three years ago.

"I am working at the Royce-Fedders tomato packing shed as a grader. My brother-in-law, Balde
Cordero, work there too. He pack tomatoes and don't
get pay for the hour, he get pay for what he pack
and since I am a grader I make sure he get the same
class tomato and that way he pack faster; he just
get a tomato with the right hand, and he wrap it
with the left. He pack a lug of tomatoes so fast
you don't see it, and he does it fast because I am
a good grader.

"Balde is a good man. His father, Don Albino, my
father-in-law who die up in Saginaw, Michigan, when
Marta and I, you know, go together . . . well, Balde
is like Don Albino, you understand? A good man. A
right man. Me, I stay an orphan and when the Mejías
take me when my father and my mother die in that
train wreck—near Flora? Don Albino tell the Mejías
I must go to the school. I go to First Ward Ele-
mentary where Mr. Gold is principal. In First Ward
I am a friend of Balde and there I meet Marta too.
Later, when I grow up I don't visit the house too

much because of Marta, you know what I mean? Anyway, Balde is my friend and I have known him very
well . . . maybe more than nobody else. He's a good
man.

"Well, last night Balde and I took a few beers
in some of the places near where we live. We drink
a couple here and a couple there, you know, and we
save the Aquí me quedo on South Missouri for last.
It is there that I tell Balde a joke about the drunk
guy who is going to his house and he hear the clock
in the corner make two sounds. You know that one?
Well, this drunk guy he hear the clock go bong-bong
and he say that the clock is wrong for it give one
o'clock two time. Well, Balde think that is funny
. . . Anyway, when I tell the joke in Spanish it's
better. Well, there we were drinking a beer when
Ernesto Tamez comes. Ernesto Tamez is like a woman,
you know? Every time he get in trouble he call his
family to help him . . . that is the way it is with
him. Well, that night he bother Balde again. More
than one time Balde has stop me when Tamez begin to
insult. That Balde is a man of patience. This time
Ernesto bring a *vieja* (woman) and Balde don't say
nothing, nothing, nothing. What happens is that
things get spooky, you know. Ernesto talking and
burlándose de él (ridiculing him) and at the same
time he have the poor woman by the arm. And then
something happen. I don't know what happen, but
something and fast.

"I don't know. I really don't know. It all happen so fast; the knife, the blood squirt all over
my face and arms, the woman try to get away, a loud
really loud scream, not a *grito* (local Mexican
yell) but more a woman screaming, you know what I
mean? and then Ernesto fall on the cement.

"Right there I look at Balde and his face is like
a mask in asleep, you understand? No angry, no surprise, nothing. In his left hand he have the knife
and he shake his head before he walk to the door.
Look, it happen so fast no one move for a while.
Then Balde come in and go out of the place and when
Don Manuel (Manuel Guzmán, constable for precinct
21) come in, Balde just hand over the knife. Lucas
Barrón, you know, El Chorreao (a nickname) well, he

wash the blood and sweep the floor before Don Manuel get there. Don Manuel just shake his head and tell Balde to go to the car and wait. Don Manuel he walk to the back to see Ernesto and on the way out one of the women, I think it is *la güera Balín* (Amelia Cortez, 23, no known address, this city), try to make a joke, but Don Manuel he say *no estés chingando* (shut the hell up, or words to that effect) and after that Don Manuel go about his own business. Me, I go to the door but all I see is Balde looking at a house across the street and he don't even know I come to say goodbye. Anyway, this morning a little boy of Don Manuel say for me to come here and here I am."

    Further deponent sayeth not.
Sworn to before me, this
17th day of March 1970

/s/ _____Helen Chacón_____   /s/ ___Gilberto Castañeda___
        Helen Chacón   Gilberto Castañeda
Acting Asst. Dpty. Recorder
Belken County

EXTRACTO DE *The Klail City Enterprise-News*
(August 24, 1970)

Klail City. (Special). Baldemar Cordero, 30, of 169 South Hidalgo
Street, drew a 15-year sentence in Judge Harrison Phelps' 139th
District Court for the murder of Ernesto Tamez last Spring to be
served in the Huntsville State Prison. PICK UP.

Cordero is alleged to have fatally stabbed Ernesto Tamez, also 30,
over the affections of one of the "hostesses" who works there.
PICK UP.

No appeal had been made at press time.

Vidas y milagros

PARA EMPEZAR, UNA DEDICATORIA

A fin de cuentas, este mundo es como una botica: hay un poco de todo. Altos, bajos, llorones, valientes, gordos, flacos, buenos, malos, listos y pendejos, unos enclenques, otros rebosantes de salud. El escritor, sin permiso de nadie, se sale a la calle y escoge de todo un poco. No se dude que de todo haya un poco y no se confunda creyendo que haya mucho de todo —a ver, ¿cuántos Napoleones ha habido? ¿O Hitlers? ¿O Jesucristos? Dejemos esto para volver a ello más adelante.

Hay gente que teme tanto cometer una falta en sociedad (enseñar la oreja, meter la pata, mearse el lado del pantalón) que, a la hora de la hora, no se atreve a nada. Esos, como temen errar, no llegarán a probar la honrada comida de una boda chicana de rancho donde, gracias a Dios, se vale todo. (Se vale todo en el sentido de que uno está entre amigos y conocidos y es mejor no andar con melindres que, al fin y al cabo, resultan ser insinceros.)

Bien. Hasta la fecha ha habido sólo un Napoleón (o un Romeo o un Raskolnikov); los tres, en diversos sentidos, se asemejan y ¿dónde empieza y termina la ficción del primero y ¿dónde la de los dos últimos? Me parece inútil el tratar de revestirlos con otros nombres y otras ropas: El chango en camisa de seda . . . Eso de trazar a alguien conocido es como jactarse de abrir brecha en camino trillado algo que viene siendo casi tan ruin como pensar en otra mujer mientras le hacemos el amor a la propia.

La originalidad, metal difícil de asir como el azogue, quizá no toque tampoco en los hombres por aquello de que de barro venimos, etc. A fin de cuentas, otra vez, somos y no somos iguales como han reconocido tantos otros.

De paso. Esa gente curiosa que se divierte con datos científicos y que tiene el afán de explicarlo todo, tiene todo el derecho de vivir y de decir lo que se le ocurra. De su parte, por supuesto, esa gente debe dejar de andar jodiendo al público por la muy buena razón de que tanto se lleva el cántaro al agua . . . En el mundo hay pasto para todos, no empujen.

Lo que sigue se dedica a la gente de Belken County y a sus espejos que los ven buenos, enfermos, en pelota, llorando, etc., de noche y de día.

ASÍ SE CUMPLE

No lejos de Bascom está el cementerio mexicano; allí en un octubre más frío de la cuenta enterraron a Pioquinto Reyes. Fue una cosa escueta y como el tiempo no daba para más, la gente acurrucada en grupitos y con la cabeza agachada defendiéndose contra la llovizna, se desparramaba con prisa hasta abandonar el lugar para otra ocasión. En el Valle, como en todas partes, el frío y la muerte suelen venir a deshora.

El difunto Pioquinto, a pesar de su nombre, era presbiteriano. En su juventud había sido demasiado serio y luego, más tarde, se hizo viejo antes de que llegara ni a los cuarenta. Hay gente que nace así, marcada y señalada como quién diga: tú vas a ser así, tu asá y tú asado; en fin, lo de siempre, el hombre propone y la tierra se lo come. A Pioquinto le tocó morir en el motel Holiday Inn que está en la carretera once enfrente de lo que fue, en mejor vida quizá, el límite del barrio de los negros.

El Pioquinto no trabajaba en el motel: estaba de huésped; el Pioquinto trabajaba como contador en que Ávila Hnos. (al mayoreo y menudeo; se reparte en casa). El Pioquinto, cuando oyó el trompetazo anunciando su día de juicio, estaba montado sobre Viola Barragán, mujer que, hace veinte años, fue carne de cañón de lo mejor, y, ahora, todavía da qué decir. El Pioquinto estiró la pata, es un decir, en plena acción, entregando el arpa como cualquier hijo de vecino.

Cuenta Rafa Buenrostro que él, de chico, asistió al entierra del hombre y, de paso, conoció a unos parientes Buenrostro en Bascom. Los Buenrostro vinieron de Querétaro al Valle cuando lo de Escandón. Entre los Buenrostro hay pobres y ricos y otros que ni tanto, como decía don Víctor Peláez. Sucede que después del entierro y cuando la gente ya se había colado, una mujer con su buen abrigo de gamuza y sombrerito de piel con velo de oreja a oreja se dirigió al montón de tierra donde descansaba el Pioquinto. De su bolsa negra de charol extrajo un pañuelo del cual estuvo deshaciendo un nudo hasta desatarlo para producir un anillo de oro que ni ancho ni grueso. Tuvo que ensuciar los guantes al enterrar el anillo al pie del montón de tierra pero ni pareció darle mayor importancia al lodo que se formaba entre el tejemaneje de los terrones y la llovizna persistente. Nada de rezos ni lloriqueos sino, más bien, una mirada resignada con la frente alta, la vista despejada, y sin la menor mueca traidora en la boca.

Según Rafa Buenrostro, Viola, viuda por primera vez a los dieciocho años poco antes de la segunda guerra mundial (en lo que va de siglo) tocaba el piano bastante mal y cantaba canciones que nadie conocía. Se había casado con un nacional de Agualeguas, Nuevo León, expatriado médicocirujano que vino a morir a manos de un boticario que ejercía sin título.

A los siete meses Viola se arrimó con don Javier Leguizamón, dueño de esos terrenos en Edgerton que, por no despreciar, se los había quitado tanto a la raza como a los bolillos. Esto duró hasta que Viola, frisando los veinte o veintiún años, fue reemplazada por Gela Maldonado, pero esto es otra historia. Con este rompimiento, la viudita se despabiló.

Después de lo de don Javier, Viola se volvió a casar; esta vez con un alemán agregado al consulado general en Tampico, Tamaulipas, que había cruzado la frontera a Estados Unidos en plan de paseo y que volvió con Viola cruzados de brazo. De Tampico la pareja zarpó para la India donde el esposo iba como primer secretario al embajador alemán. La guerra mundial, como ya se sabe, echó la cosa al traste y así fue como Viola Barragán, muchacha originaria de Ruffing, Texas, hija de Telésforo Barragán y Felícitas Surís de Barragán, fue a parar en un campo de concentración inglés en las afueras de Calcutta. Me la tuvieron en la sombra al lado de su señor esposo hasta que se les trasladó a Pretoria en la república sudafricana donde les sorprendió la rendición del coronel-general Jodl en una escuela de primaria de aquel oscuro pueblecito francés.

El esposo de Viola no perdió ripio; se volvió a Alemania y, ni corto ni perezoso, en menos de cinco años ya estaba de nuevo en Pretoria como funcionario de la Volkswagen Werke y, por supuesto, con Viola a su lado. Andando el tiempo, el alemán muere de repente, le deja a Viola sus buenos pesos, ésta vuelve a Estados Unidos y, como los mismos pajaritos a su nido, cae en Belken County.

De vuelta a su pueblo natal encontró que Telésforo y Felícitas se habían mudado a Edgerton. Allá les cayó Viola; se compró una casona; recogió a sus padres; no se olvidó en nada de sus parientes y conocidos; y, aparentemente, se retiró de su vida andariega y aventurera.

La gente, maravillada, no hallaba por dónde empezar y lo único que podía decir era que a Viola no se le había olvidado el español. Lo más probable es que ni se preocupó por aprender alemán; a decir verdad, en muchos casos ni se necesita hablar.

Pasando el tiempo, el diablo, ese amigo del débil, le deparó una sorpresa más a Viola Barragán en la figura de Pioquinto Reyes.

Pioquinto, seriecito, de camisa a rayas bien almidonada, se había casado con Blanca Rivera; no tuvieron hijos, pero parte para compensar y parte por aquello de que de lo perdido lo que aparezca, Blanca y el hermano Limón lograron que Pioquinto se hiciera presbiteriano. La batalla debió ser corta y con poca sangre porque al Pioquinto no le gustaba alborotar.

Cuando Viola se instaló en Edgerton, Pioquinto, seguramente, ni cuenta se dio. Lo que pasó fue que un buen día, Viola, que con tiempo y dinero de sobra, acostumbraba atravesar el Valle en carro desde Edgerton a Jonesville-on-the-River, iba por Bascom en aquel carrazo color guindo cuando divisó a Pioquinto por vez primera. Al catarlo con esa cara seria y santona, Viola dijo para sí, "Éste es de los míos; ahora hago lo que hago porque me da la gana y no por comer caliente". Y así fue como el diablo los juntó hasta que Dios, meses más tarde, los separó en el motel.

Cuando el Pioquinto petateó en el Holiday Inn, Viola (que ya no se asustaba de nada) se vistió sin prisa desocupando el cuarto para salir gallardamente rumbo a Edgerton donde se desentendió del caso como si tal cosa. Al Pioquinto se lo encontró una secatrapos que aviso al gerente que etc. y etc.

Lo sepultaron en el cementerio mexicano de Bascom; su afligida esposa y demás familiares le rogaron al Señor que viera por su alma y que lo recogiera en su seno por los siglos de los siglos, amén. Los feligreses presbiterianos del Buen Pastor Church en la calle nueve hicieron todo a la mano.

¿Viola? Regular, gracias, y ahora a los cincuenta y pico de años todavía se defiende bastante bien contra el tiempo. Lo del anillo, ni para qué decirlo, fue un gesto de primera, un gesto de desprendimiento digno de enseñanza a los de poco corazón.

LOS REVOLUCIONARIOS

Se acaban los revolucionarios. En el condado de Belken, en el Valle, quedan pocos; unos libres y otros, con menos fortuna, prisioneros en esas rest homes de las que nadie se salva. Esos, los de las rest homes, en efecto, ya no son revolucionarios; son cartuchos quemados, parque mojado que no rinde chispa. Son como las balas Mauser en los rifles Springfield: inservibles. Ese es el caso.

Los otros, los libres, se están acabando también, salvo que ellos saben todavía muy bien quiénes son y qué fueron. Como están libres, se juntan de noche a madrugada en la banca de la esquina y platican de esto y aquello cada vez puliendo, mejorando sus historias mientras que la memoria (esa novia infiel) les echa zancadilla de vez en cuando. Sin embargo, son incansables; vuelven a la carga tal y como lo hicieron en las filas de Villa, de Lucio Blanco y de los hermanos Arrieta en San Pedro de las Colonias, Culiacán, Celaya . . .

Estos viejitos como don Braulio Tapia, Evaristo Garrido y don Manuel Guzmán, nacieron en Estados Unidos pero guerrearon en la Revolución igual que tantos otros de la misma camada y calaña, como se dice. Los padres de esta gente también nacieron en este país así como los abuelos (aquí se habla ya de 1765 y antes). Como la tierra era igual para los méxicoamericanos dada la proximidad a las fronteras y el bolón de parientes en ambos lados que nunca distinguieron entre tierra y río, el atravesar la una y cruzar el otro lo mismo era, fue y (aunque los de la inmigración —la migra— no lo crean) sigue siendo igual para muchos méxicoamericanos; la raza, pues, hacía lo que le daba la gana con su vida.

Los padres y tíos que criaron a estos revolucionarios también guerrearon y fueron revolucionarios (los sediciosos como se les llamaba), sólo que lo fueron acá, en su propio país, en lo que se viene llamando Estados Unidos de América.

Esto de ser revolucionario le puede tocar a cualquiera pero, como en todas las cosas, son pocos los escogidos. Son algo así como el ganado ajeno que va y viene, cambia de marca y dueño pero, al fin, lo de siempre: vienen el tiempo y la jodencia, y apaga la luz que ya nos vamos.

I

Braulio Tapia, natural de El Esquilmo (ahora, Skidmore) Texas, nació en agosto de 1883; a Braulio lo criaron Juan Nepomuceno Celaya y una tía materna, Barbarita Farías de Celaya, ambos de Goliad, Texas, donde el que sustituyó al gral. Urrea hizo pasar por las armas al coronel Fannin y a otros insurgentes durante la rebelión de Texas en 1835-36.

Braulio apareció en lo que es ahora Belken County en 1908 y se casó dos años después con Sóstenes Calvillo, hija única de don Práxedis Calvillo y Albinita Buenrostro. De este matrimonio nació Matilde; ésta se casó con don Jehú Vilches y tuvieron una hija, María Teresa de Jesús, que se casó con Roque Malacara. Al llegar a esta última generación, las tierras y propiedades que la raza sostenía en la región ya pertenecían, en muy gran parte, a los bolillos; la raza que llegó a quedarse con tierra se podía dividir casi en dos partes: en primer lugar, los más viejos que se formaron en contra de los bolillos en trámites de sí-y-no (aunque también corrió la sangre); y en segundo lugar, los otros, los ansiosos, o sea, la raza que se granjeó con la bolillada para comerse las sobras en forma de tierra que les dejaban los montoneros, los políticos y los abogados.

Cuando Braulio Tapia habla con sus amigos, habla más de lo que hizo su padre de crianza, don Juan Ene, que lo que él, Braulio, le tocó hacer en la Revolución. Es rara la vez que se queje pero cuando lo hace es por las piernas donde lleva dos o tres balas (no se acuerda ya del número exacto) que por poco lo aplastan durante el sitio de San Pedro de las Colonias. Cuando le da la gana se pone a cantar aquello de:

San Pedro de las Colonias;
que lejos te vas quedando
¡quedando!

Un pariente de Braulio, aunque difícil de descifrar la parentela, es Evaristo Garrido.

II

Evaristo nunca se casó pero dejó sucesión: dos hijos por Andreíta Cano (de Ruffing), el Pascual que se murió en la tifoidea del '16 y Andrés que salió tonto. También, una muchachita de Petrita San Miguel: la Natalia que se casó con Sotero Garza Parás, originario de Cadereyta Jiménez, Nuevo León.

Los Vilches, los Garrido y los Malacara viejos se aliaron para sostener las tierras contra los rinches, primero en el rancho Toluca de los Vilches, cerca de Relámpago, y luego, durante toda una semana santa, en el rancho del Carmen, en las tierras de don Jesús Buenrostro, "El Quieto". Después de estos dos encontronazos los rinches se dejaron de estar molestando.

En otras ocasiones y en otros lugares, la raza perdió tierra y gente, legalmente y a traición. A los muertos, ni se diga, les importa poco el cómo y el dónde.

Cuando el tiroteo en Toluca, varios parientes del otro lado cruzaron el río para ayudar a la raza aunque no compartieron en el combate. Cruzaron porque unos que dizque "voluntarios" de la caballería americana habían acampado cerca del terreno de los Vilches y Malacara; como los parientes no eran dejados, se quedaron a ver qué hacían los soldados mientras los rinches y la gente de Toluca estaban en lo suyo. Así se quedó la cosa hasta que la soldadesca se volvió a Fort Jones en Jonesville-on-the-River. Los parientes los siguieron a la distancia por el lado mexicano.

Evaristo estuvo en Culiacán y en Matamoros con Lucio Blanco. Durante el bombardeo de Matamoros, Evaristo fue a visitar a unos parientes en las Yescas que está al otro lado de Relámpago, Texas: allí conoció a la Petrita San Miguel. En Culiacán, tiempo atrás, no le había ido tan bien: dejó la mano derecha, con todos los dedos, en el estado de Sinaloa; granada de mano que reventó antes de tiempo.

III

Don Manuel Guzmán llegó a conocer a Villa y a Obregón, en persona. Empezó vendiéndole caballos al primero y acabo enrolándose en las filas del segundo como zapador. Dejó a Villa después de las refriegas en Celaya; volvió primero a Flora y, al poco tiempo, se mudó a Klail City. Allí se estuvo varios meses: se casó, compró terreno y volvió a la carga formando parte del ejército constitucional en el distrito militar de Papantla, Veracruz. De ahí su larga amistad con don Víctor Peláez.

Don Manuel se casó con doña Josefa Carrión huérfana de Julián Carrión y María del Pilar Sifuentes, ambos muertos en un ataque por unos apaches bandoleros en Seago Point, Texas. Doña Josefa fue una mujer fuerte. Amó a su esposo, nunca le dio guerra, no le molesto con el-qué-dirán y le crió cinco hijos: dos de ellos y tres que aparecieron en su casa un sábado de gloria. No se sabe por qué escogieron esa casa de tantas en la vecindad pero se les crió como hijos y, de suerte, todos salieron bien.

El hombre conoció a Obregón y parece que le cayó bien al sonorense porque se le nombró oficial primero de carceleros en Lecumberri. Las cosas iban bien y cuando estaba pensando en traerse a la familia para México, Toral de León asesina a Obregón en La Bombilla y don Manuel abandona la idea de quedarse en la capital. Vuelve a Klail por un rato y se da cuenta que ha perdido el terreno que había comprado. Doña Josefa, a pesar de su fuerza, no le llegaba a la punta de los pies al papelaje que le encajaron los land developers.

Don Manuel no rajó. Se hizo domador de caballos en que los Tuero. (Allí, precisamente, le dio en la madre a Javier Leguiza-món, padre, que en ese tiempo la hacía de correiveidile a los Cooke, a los Blanchard y a los Klail.) Más tarde don Manuel tuvo una lechería y tres sastrerías, dos en Flora, otra en Ruffing. Con el dinero que hizo ayudó a muchos amigos revolucionarios más necesitados que él. Andando el tiempo, don Domingo Villalobos hizo que a don Manuel lo nombraran policía en Klail City, en el barrio mexicano. Así todos salieron bien: los bolillos porque no tenían que molestarse con la raza, y la raza misma que, en don Manuel, hallaron a todo un hombre.

Leía y escribía lo que se dice bien; el inglés lo chapuceaba pero siendo hombre discreto no se metía mucho en ese idioma.

Las vidas de don Manuel fueron en español.

Ahora ya le fallan los ojos pero el ánimo no y mientras haya amigos . . .

UN DOMINGO EN KLAIL

¡Vamosay! ¡Vamosay! ¡Cuadro . . . ánimo en el cuadro!
¡Vamosay, palomilla, nobody hurt, nobody hurt! ¡Vamosay!
El que grita se llama Arturo Leyva:

Tenedor de libros de profesión;
fanático de béisbol por afición;
a los cuatro sufrió de sarampión;
y en la escuela le llamaban el Cagón.

Arturo no entiende muy bien eso de "nobody hurt" pero lo
repite porque es algo que ha oído desde niño. Esto no quiere decir
que Arturo no sepa inglés; al contrario, se defiende bastante bien.
Sin embargo, eso de "nobody hurt" sigue siendo un misterio.

Arturo está en el parque Leones viendo al 30-30 de Klail en un
double-header contra el Sox de Flora. Está reñido el combate;
Lázaro "Skinny" Peña no ha permitido un hit (ni a su madre, si a
doña Estela se le ocurriera arrimarse con un bate al plato). La cosa
se va poniendo buena. La pelota es uno de los pocos lujos que se
permite Arturo.

Hasta los pájaros saben que Arturo es esposo de Yolanda Salazar, hija única de don Epigmenio el que se relajó antes de la guerra mundial número dos. (Este relajo es estrictamente médico; el
otro, el moral, lo ha tenido desde que respira.) Arturo es aliado de
su suegro contra doña Candelaria Munguía de Salazar. El Arturo
tal vez ignora que el doctor Nicola Machiavelli haya existido pero
ha intuido que la fuerza está en la alianza.

La alianza es de rigor porque doña Candelaria es muy déspo-
ta. Arturo, no obstante, va a lo suyo y andando. Con Yolanda no
hay mitotes, Arturo le lleva el pulso.

Entre la gente en el parque Leones está Manzur Chajín, dulcero libanes aunque la gente le llama "el árabe". Chajín vive en el

barrio y está casado con chicana (Catarina de León). A los dos meses de casados ésta ya sabía hacer esos dulces redondos color colorado con cacahuates; la cosa, es verdad, no tiene mayor gracia pero algo es algo. Chajín, como cualquier hijo de su país, pronuncia la *p* como si fuera *b* y cuando habla de don Manuel dice que es tan buen *bolicia* que no necesita *bistola*. Chajín no vende dulces en el parque; se lo deja a los chicos que para eso es el patrón.

Arturo fue a hacer la chi y ya está de vuelta. Mientras tanto, Skinny se ha chiflado en forma exagerada: van ocho entradas y todavía no ha permitido hit (ni a su madre, ni a doña Estela, etc.).

¡Vamosay, 30-30! ¡Vamosay!

Arturo.

¿Qué?

No, nada. Descuida . . .

Allí viene don Manuel Guzmán: él no entiende mucho de la pelota aunque reconoce que no cualquiera puede meterse en ese juego serio. Hace un calorón (estamos en agosto) pero don Manuel, como siempre, va de camisa blanca con ligas en las mangas y de corbata negra. Y, también como siempre, lleva ese reloj suizo con leontina de oro, artículos que le tocaron como parte de la herencia de don Víctor Peláez.

¡Arturo!

Sí, don Manuel, diga.

Yolanda se acaba de ir. Dice que la recojas en que tu suegra.

Sí, señor, gracias.

Arturo Leyva está más a gusto. Ama a Yolanda, sí, y ni se le ocurriría echarse querida —¡quite Ud.! —pero la pelota es la pelota y— ¡qué caray! —no todos los días son domingo. El Skinny no ha permitido hit y vamos a la décima entrada: lo malo es que el Sox de Flora tiene dos hermanos negros como batería: el Mann Moore de pitcher y su hermano Clyde, de catcher; para que más se descomponga el asunto, el 30-30 de Klail es lo que los conocidos llaman good field, no hit.

Arturo, aunque tenedor de libros, es resistente: esta noche, después del partido, llevara a Yolanda al baile en la calle Hidalgo y, luego, más tarde, al catre, porque además de resistente es cumplidor.

Me parece que ya se dijo que le lleva el pulso a la Yolanda.

LOS LEGUIZAMÓN

Los primeros Leguizamón llegaron a Belken County en 1865, después de atole, como quien dice, y se asentaron en lo que son ahora Bascom y parte de Flora. Más tarde se extendieron al norte, hacia Ruffing, y al oeste, hacia Jonesvilleon-the-River. En un tiempo concertaron casamientos con los Calvillo, los Surís y los Celaya pero no se firmaron contratos ni nada.

Los casamientos se disolvieron por esas cosas que pasan. Vino otra generación de Leguizamón y éstos fueron los que acapararon la tierra mencionada; otra generación perdió parte y todavía otra se concentró en retenerla hasta el presente.

Los primeros Leguizamón supieron defenderse solos a puro pulso contra la bolillada que vino al Valle con la Biblia en una mano y el garrote en la otra.

Cinco salieron de la presente generación —todos hijos de Clemente Leguizamón que murió en Freitas ayudando a los rinches en contra de los Vilches y los Malacara. Clemente enviudó dos veces: primero de Carmelita Hennington, que según la raza, era cuarterona —todo puede ser; y, en segunda viudez, con Diamantina Lerdo; los cinco Leguizamón, pues, son Leguizamón-Lerdo. Diamantina murió bien loca; la mordió un perro rabioso, después de misa, durante aquella canícula feroz de 1904, año en el que no llovió un sólo día en el condado de Belken. (Ese mismo año, siete carretas repletas de gente, rosarios y provisión, salieron de Klail City y Edgerton rumbo a San Juan de los Lagos, Jalisco, a rezarle a la Virgen para que lloviera en Belken. En este viaje nació Julián Buenrostro, hermano menor de Jesús, "El Quieto".)

Los Hennington desaparecieron como vinieron, sin aviso; hay gente que cree que se fueron a Veracruz. Los Lerdo vinieron al Valle con los Buenrostro cuando don José de Escandón encandiló a medio mundo en Querétaro; la sangre de los Lerdo salió rala, ni un duro arriba de los 50 años. (Esa raza no daba para más. El cruce con los Leguizamón ayudó al apellido Lerdo pero no fue gran cosa.)

Los Leguizamón-Lerdo, o Leguizamón, a secas, fueron cinco, como se ha dicho: 1) César que murió a los 45 en 1927, balaceado por los rinches mismos que tanto había ayudado cuando los zafarranchos de 1901-1903; los de 1906-1907; y el último de 1923; 2) Alejandro, mujeriego y jugador pero nada cobarde, que también se alió con la bolillada y así logró ser recompensado con esas tierras cerca de Ruffing. A Alejandro se lo encontraron agonizando un domingo en la madrugada en el patio de la iglesia del Sagrado Corazón de Jesús; le habían sumido los sesos con una espátula; 3) Antonia que se casó con uno de los Blanchard ricos y cuyos hijos salieron bolillos; 4) Javier y Martín, gemelos, que se apoderaron de las tierras en Edgerton. Martín murió quemado en alcohol; Javier es el único de los hombres que vive y ya no es tan joven como él se cree aunque se pinte el pelo.

A Javier, de joven, don Manuel Guzmán, también joven, le rompió las narices por metiche y encimoso; fue una tarde de doma de caballos en el rancho de los Tuero. En esos tiempos Javier Leguizamón pertenecía al bando de la raza que se granjeaba con los bolillos. Tuvo buenos resultados, recibió bastante tierra en la punta oeste del condado.

Se casó con Angelita Villalobos, hija de don Domingo Villalobos que consiguió hacer las paces en el Valle tanto por su valentía como por su talento. Don Domingo fue el que le puso el apodo de "Chinga Quedito" a su yerno; se ve que ni en pintura lo quería ver.

Andando el tiempo, Javier también acaparó varias tiendas de ropas y abarrotes y, en una de ellas, trabajó Jehú Malacara de chico-para-todo: dependiente, cartero, mensajero, barrendero . . . Además de tierras, Javier acaparó queridas. Entre ellas, a Viola Barragán, recién viuda y cuando estaba como tren, y a la Gela Maldonado que le exprimió sus buenos pesos y, de paso, instaló su propia tienda. Claro; ya sabía el negocio por dentro y por fuera. Esta unión Leguizamón-Maldonado duro cosa de doce años.

La historia de los Leguizamón viejos quizá interese más pero este no es el lugar de ellos. De los cinco que hablamos sólo quedan dos, Antonia y Javier. Como en todas familias, hay un poco de todo. Estos dos ni se ven ni se hablan. Creo que la Antonia no quiere acordarse de su sangre chicana pero eso le ocurre a muchos y qué le vamos a hacer. Javier no es chicano tampoco, es Leguizamón y los Leguizamón, bien es sabido, no tuvieron madre; fueron hijos de tía.

BETO CASTAÑEDA

Muerto en su casa en 169 South Hidalgo, en Klail City, condado de Belken, Beto Castañeda, esposo de Marta Cordero de Castañeda, a la edad de treinta años. Hombre trabajador, recibió escasa escuela formal pero llegó a conocer la tierra y sus productos como un catedrático debe conocer su materia si es que se precie.

Los padres de Beto murieron en aquel accidente en Flora cuando un tren de carga mató a unas veinte personas, entre ellos los padres de Beto. (En menos de una semana, los Ayala habían escrito un corrido que cobró mucha fama entre la raza. La imprenta Acosta lo imprimió y el maestro Barrientos le puso música. El disco se grabó por Águila Records en Corpus Christi.) La familia, Beto incluso, iba a la yerba cuando al troque se le apagó el motor en medio de los rieles y entonces resultó la matanza.

A Beto lo recogieron los Mejía y a los siete años asistió al First Ward, la escuela de la raza, porque el difunto don Albino Cordero les dijo a los Mejía que educaran al muchacho. Como se sabe, andando el tiempo, y muchos años después, Beto se casó con Marta, hija única de don Albino.

A los quince años Beto Castañeda ya había hecho no menos de seis viajes al norte: uno con Víctor Jara, El Pirulí, que se portó mal y medio robó a la gente quedándose con buena parte del dinero que la Skinner Produce Company había dado como adelanto. El dinero se mandaba a un banco en San Antonio, el troquero lo recibía y debía repartirlo a la gente dando tanto y tanto por cabeza. El Pirulí repartió el dinero, sí, pero no todo, ni cómo debía: que no se vayan a creer que el resto se lo volvió a la Skinner Produce.

Beto hizo dos viajes con Sabas Balderas; uno a la cherry en Benton Harbor y St. Joseph, Mich.; el segundo lo realizó a Traverse City, también en Michigan y también a la cherry. Tres viajó en los troques de Cantú Hnos., el último como asistente de chofer: ya manejaba un poco y como hablaba inglés allanaba el camino en la ruta Klail City-Texarkana Poplar Bluff-Kankakee-New Buffalo, Michigan. Serio sin ser orgulloso ni reservado, murió de cáncer a los treinta años de edad. Con él murió el último testigo de lo que realmente pasó en el Aquí Me Quedo hará ya un par de años. La familia del muerto, los Tamez, nunca lo molestaron a él por lo ocurrido; Balde Cordero, su cuñado, sigue alzado en Sugarland y, ahora, con la muerte de Beto, se quedan Marta y doña Mercedes Cordero solas.

No recuerdo que alguien le haya ganado a empacar cualquier tipo de la verdura que llaman gruesa y pesada (brécol, betabel, espárrago, espinaca, lechuga, pepino); una vez, cuando tendría unos diecinueve años, en competencia con Chale Villalón, que contaría con veinticuatro, Beto le dio caja y media de ventaja en el empaque y corte de lechuga. Al fin de cuatro horas, Beto empató y salió ganando con tres cuartos de caja. Por su parte, Beto contaba que el mejor empacador de tomate era su cuñado, Balde Cordero. Puede ser. Dicen que el viejo Zepúlveda era de lo mejor pero no valía la cuenta porque le entraba a la grifa y así cualquiera.

En todo el Valle sólo hubo dos hombres que le ganaron a hacer pulso, el primero fue Ismael Contreras, que jamás le perdió a nadie, y el segundo, Chago Lerma, de Ruffing, que pulsaba tan bien con la derecha como con la izquierda.

Se le despidió en el cementerio católico mexicano en Klail y los Vega estuvieron encargados del entierro. El orador fue don Rosendo Estapa, el que trabaja con la ciudad.

Beto Castañeda, 1941-1971, amigo cabal, q.e.p.d.

COYOTES

se les llama a esos que se dejan ver en la sede del condado, el county court house, como quien dice. No son empleados aunque lo parezcan: se visten de camisa blanca y corbata o, si son mujeres, de zapato con tacón alto y de media larga. Afanan en los pasillos diariamente y viven de lo que le suelten al pobre que se asome en la corte con algún negocio. Tampoco son abogados pero como hablan inglés, claro es, ya tienen ventaja. Están al tanto de cualquier runrún en la corte y como desconocen la vergüenza, se ponen las botas con cada inocente que les caiga. La gente que no sabe nada de nada se asusta de cualquier sobre con sello oficial y por eso es ganado bastante fácil para los coyotes.

Adrián Peralta, coyote, es de Edgerton y viaja de allí a Klail de diario. Trigueño, sombrero de petate a la moda, camisa blanca y corbata con ganchito de donde salta un pez vela, sonrisa en la boca que no en los ojos, bigote fifí, con ese par de ojos mencionados que si no han visto todo poco les falta. Como tiene la piel curtida ya no le entran ni indirectas ni insultos. Tiene buena representación y mejor voz ya que hasta la fecha nadie le ha rompido las narices. Es muy democrático, según él, y allí se le puede ver saludando a todo mundo, altos y bajos, hembras y machos, jueces y reos, putas y queridos, etc.

¿En qué puedo servirle?

Psss, verá usté, aquí traigo este papel . . . me cayó por correo y como dice Court House . . . aquí estoy, ya ve.

Adrián Peralta, un servidor. ¿Su gracia?

Marcial de Anda, señor. (Don Marcial debe tener unos 70 años: es dulcero de profesión. Tiene cuatro hijos: Juan, Emerardo, Marcial hijo, y Jovita, la que se tuvo que casar con Joaquín Tamez. De esto ya hace tiempo.)

¿Me permite?

Sí, señor.

Primero, un mmmmmmmmmmmmmmmmmmm largo, reservado
y lleno de misterio. Luego una mirada a don Marcial y, al momento, otra al papel. Le toma el sobre, introduce la carta en él, lleva a
don Marcial del codo y se presenta en una oficina. Nada. Luego a
otra donde también pregunta por tal y tal; no, no está aquí. Gracias.
Entran a la tercera y aquí es donde te quiero ver, pichón.
Amigo de Anda, voy a arreglarle este asunto en un dos por tres.
Hablando de un dos por tres, ¿me puede pasar un par de dólares
para hacer andar la maquinaria? Ya sabe que sin grasa no se puede
caminar.

Coge el dinero, le vuelve el sobre y antes de despedirse le seña-
la una ventanita. Allí mero, dice, pregunte por Miss Espinoza, una
muchacha bien peinada. Como es raza y no tiene pena de serlo,
Miss Espinoza sonríe a don Marcial y le saluda en español. Es la
oficina del County Tax Assessor y a don Marcial le han nombrado
para el jurado; no, no tiene que presentarse ahora; no, que no se
reunirán hasta el fin de año; no, no me debe nada que aquí estamos
para servirlo . . . Miss Espinoza le advierte que no ande dando su
dinero a los coyotes.

Como don Marcial no tiene que pagar nada se siente feliz
—tanto que ni se acuerda ya de los dos billetes que le sacó el coyote; ni por pienso que vaya a seguir el consejo de la muchacha. Don
Marcial vuelve a su casa en paz, hasta la próxima.

Peralta ahora está tomando café en el coffee lounge. Está de
pie, por si acaso. Como ya hizo la cruz con don Marcial se siente
a gusto y está listo para caerle encima a otro inocente que venga a
la corte con ese susidio de la raza tan conocido.

Buenos días, señora. Adrián Peralta, un servidor, para ayudar-
le en lo que se pueda . . .

BURNIAS

Mucha gente no lo cree, pero la suerte, así como el tiempo y la memoria, viene y va. Hay unos que la tienen buena, otros que les cae mala y hay otros todavía que se adueñan de una suerte infinitamente más negra que la sombra del canelón. Melitón Burnias, a todas luces, es uno de estos últimos. Como Melitón no corta figura trágica, la gente, claro es, lo toma a choteo. Burnias vive como puede y sin tratar de molestar; lo que pasa es que vive en Flora y esa gente mitotera no le deja a usted ni el resuello. A veces, a Burnias se le ponen las cosas color de hormiga, como cuando lo echaron de la casa su hija Tila y el yerno, Práxedis Cervera. (Este Burnias, en otra ocasión, fue el socio de Bruno Cano en la busca de tesoro.)

También de Flora es Martín Lalanda, comerciante, rentero, exsocio de la barbería El Rizo de Oro y dueño de un camión que usa para llevar o, según, traer grava. Es uno de esos troques marca International que en el Valle llaman "chatos".

Lo que sigue, pues, ocurrió hace unos ocho años:

Lalanda empleó a Burnias —haciéndole un favor— para que manejara el camión de grava, pero cuando el de la compañía de seguros se dio cuenta que era Burnias el chofer, se fue corriendo a ver a Lalanda y le avisó: o quita usted a Burnias como chofer o le retiramos el seguro. (Ni para que negarlo, Burnias tenía cuenta abierta y corriente con el departamento de seguridad pública.) Lalanda no tuvo más remedio; no es un mal hombre aunque sí algo tacaño y agarrado con su dinero (Don Víctor Peláez, hombre ocurrente, le puso el apodo "El Cañón de Bachimba" porque nunca disparaba).

Así que destituyeron a Burnias, pareció que el cielo se le venía encima otra vez. Lalanda bien sabía que Burnias no tenía dónde parar y le dijo que podía vivir en la cabaña del camión. Así es que la máquina andaba para arriba y abajo todo el santo día y, de noche, servía de casa y techo para Burnias.

210

Ocurre que un buen día, el viejo Chandler, de Relámpago, necesitaba una manita en las tierras y Burnias se fue allá. El trabajo era corto (tres días) pero jodedor (16 horas diarias) y así fue que empezó en un viernes muy temprano y acabó en un domingo bastante tarde. Al cumplir con el trabajo, el viejo Chandler arregló sus cuentas con el jornalero y le pagó, pero no con dinero sino en especie: le pagó con un marrano. Un cuino de color entre zaino y colorado.

Hain't got the money, Burnias. All I got's the pig; you take him.

De perdido, lo que aparezca. Se vinieron Burnias y su marrano a la cabaña del International y allí le arregló, lo mejor que pudo, un chiquero de vigas de ferrocarril. El marrano, tan manso que parecía perro capado, se echó a roncar como un angelito de Dios. A la madrugada vinieron el chofer y Lalanda; éste vio a la pareja y despertó al que hablaba.

La cosa se explicó fácilmente y entonces fue cuando Burnias le pidió dos dólares a Lalanda: los necesito para comprar maíz. Le doy de comer el maíz, lo engordo en unos cuantos días, lo relleno con un poco de agua y lo revendo. Oyendo esto último Lalanda aflojó la lana y Burnias empezó a hacer lo suyo.

Dicho y hecho: el zaino empezó a verse bien y a los diez días ya se veía redondito por su dieta de maíz y toda el agua que resistiera. Lalanda se quedó de una pieza y creyó ver un talento latente en Melitón Burnias que hasta allí ni había sospechado. Llegó el jueves y entre los dos subieron al cochino al troque de grava y se dirigieron a la venta de animales en Klail City.

Al llegar, metieron al marrano en el baño desinfectante y así, limpiecito por fuera, se lo presentaron al veterinario federal, un jovel él, flaco, con lentes cafés y pecas del mismo color, y de saco blanco que le daba a las rodillas. Le abrió la boca al marrano, le vio la lengua, anduvo alrededor y se agachó: le tocó el pene haciendo que el marrano se meara dentro de un frasquito que contenía un líquido color verde claro. Rodeó de nuevo al animal y, a cada paso, batiendo el frasco con el líquido y las aguas menores del zaino. Serían dos minutos o algo así cuando el líquido se puso de un verde oscuro y allá fue donde el veterinario le avisó a Burnias que sorry, sir, but this pig's sick. Can't sell him.

¿Pero pos why?

Pig's got worms in his kidney; a disease called *Stephanarus dentatus*. Know what I mean? Best thing to do is to kill him and bury him. Can't sell him.

Burnias vió a Lalanda y éste a aquel y, sin media palabra, subieron su carga al camión otra vez y vámonos de aquí que no nos quieren.

Te digo, Melitón, tú siempre andas tan de malas que hasta los perros te mean.

Sí, y no digo perros; hasta los marranos.

Lalanda, sin malicia, se rió y Burnias, resignado, también. Pusieron la máquina en marcha y los dos, sin hablar y entre cigarro y cigarro, se quedaron con la vista al frente cosa de media hora. Por fin, Lalanda rompió fuego:

Mira, Melitón, vamos a Relámpago y se lo vendemos al viejo Chandler.

Pero, señor Lalanda, si yo conseguí el marrano del viejo Chandler mismo.

Por eso: vamos y tratamos de vendérselo; él no lo comprará —¡qué lo va a comprar!— y entonces se lo regalamos, ¿entiendes? Sí, se lo regalamos. Tampoco lo va a querer regalado —no le vaya a contaminar los otros, ¿verdad? Bueno, nosotros nos hacemos pendejos y le decimos que si no nos lo compra que está bien, que se lo regalamos y bajamos al zaino y lo llevamos al chiquero.

Poooos, la verdad que no entiendo.

Es fácil: un regalo no se rechaza y éste, menos, porque si lo rechaza tenemos que preguntarle por qué y ¿qué cara va a poner? Así es que tiene que comprarlo. Ya comprado y siendo su propiedad puede hacer de él lo que le dé su chingada gana.

¿Usté cree?

Por esta cruz (dedo pulgar horizontal; dedo índice vertical).

❀ ❀ ❀

En efecto, el viejo Chandler se vió acorralado y soltó los veintisiete del alma que le pidieron; Lalanda cogió los dos que le había prestado a Burnias, y otro por la gasolina. Esa noche, Burnias cogió un pedo de falda afuera y de bragueta abierta en la cantina de Germán Salinas. Como no estorbaba, allí se estuvo hasta que cerraron.

No llegó a la cabaña del camión: se fue a dormir al campo de sandía. Allí, al día siguiente, despertaría con una cruda como una casa, pero tendría su medicina a la mano: el jugo dulce y refrescante de sandía serenada.

❀ ❀ ❀

Mucha gente no entiende eso de la suerte y quizá será por eso que viva de greñas y uñas, patadas y zancadillas. La gente es muy ansiosa y quiere que la suerte, para ellos, siempre sea buena. ¡No puede ser, gentes, no sean abusadores! Quizá la suerte sea más bien como una mujer: hay veces que no tiene ganas y hay veces que sí y el elegido (créanlo) ni cuenta se da.

Una vida de Rafa Buenrostro

En junio de 1944, Chano Ortega, un muchacho de Klail City, murió durante la invasión de Francia. Su madre, Tina Ruiz, viuda de Ortega, hasta la fecha, no sabe qué andaba haciendo su hijo en las Europas.

Lo que sigue es para él y para unos muy contados.

En la escuela americana, en el primer año, Miss Moy se lavaba las manos con alcohol y usaba mucho Kleenex. Tenía el pelo colorado y una cara llena de pecas. No sé cómo le hizo, pero a mí me enseñó a leer en inglés.

Un día se le ocurrió a Miss Bunn preguntarle a Lucy Ramírez que qué se había desayunado esa mañana. La muy mentiretas dijo que había tomado un vaso de orange juice y dos scrambled eggs con toast y jelly. Thank you, Lucy. Cuando le preguntó lo mismo al difunto Leo Pumarejo, el cabrón de Leo le dijo la verdad: one tortilla de harina WITH PLENTY OF PEANUT BUTTER!

A Hilario Borrego le di una trompada y sangró. Leo y yo nos habíamos apoderado de la resbaladera durante el recess y no dejábamos que subiera nadie que no fuera del barrio. Hilario vivía en el Rebaje y por eso nos peleamos. Cuando a su mamá le avisaron que le había sacado sangre, la vieja cabrona vino y me cacheteó. Yo tenía siete años y no pude aguantar, lloré un chingo. Pero no me rajé. De allí en adelante yo me las amanaba con Hilario y Leo me avisaba si venía la vieja o no.

Cuando vino el de la compañía a cortarle el agua a los Ponce porque no tenían conqué, toda la vecindad vino a ver de qué se trataba. El de la compañía, con su sonrisita, le soltó dos o tres palabras en español machacado a doña Trini. Ésta, que no hablaba inglés, le dijo al bolillo que se fuera a hacer gárgaras de cagada.

En Flora la vida no vale nada y la raza un punto menos: Cuando el estado de Texas hizo un juicio a Van Meers, después de cinco años de haber matado a Mora a balazos, y en plena calle, los testigos del estado atestiguaron a favor de Van Meers y en contra del muerto.

Una vez, en Edgerton, mi papá le dio tres tiros a uno que se le vino navaja en mano. Papá me dijo que no le dijera nada a mamá cuando volviéramos a casa y así fue. Después empecé a tartamudear y me puse muy enfermo. No sané hasta que la tía Panchita, con sus rezos y un huevo, me curó de susto.

Cada noche, cuando le ayudábamos al árabe a meter más de 200 bushels de frutas y verduras en la tienda, el muy hijo de su chingada madre nos pagaba dándonos manzanas y duraznos podridos. Y uno, de pendejo, no se quejaba.

Se murió Tacha, una señora muy vieja que vivía en el callejón. Fui con mi primo a verla allí tendida y él fue el que me mostró los pedazos de algodón que le habían puesto en la nariz y en los oídos. Olían a alcohol. Mi primo, haciéndose el gallón, entró en el cuarto donde estaba Tacha tendida y le tocó un brazo. Luego, con un centavo, hizo la señal de la cruz y me dijo que ese centavo era de la buena suerte.

A Pioquinto Reyes lo enterraron en el cementerio mexicano de Bascom. No sé por qué acompañé yo a papá al entierro y lo poco que me acuerdo era que quizá hiciera demasiado frío para el mes de octubre. Después del entierro papá me llevó a una casa donde vivían unos primos míos que yo no conocía; me dieron carne asada, tortillas de harina y café de rancho; lo sirvieron sin leche y con Karo Syrup en vez de azúcar. Unas señoras que estaban allí de visita me tocaban los ojos con la palma de las manos para que no me hicieran ojo. Yo no creía en el mal de ojo pero desde que me habían curado de susto yo ya no sabía qué pensar. . .

Una vez volvíamos mi primo y yo de la escuela cuando un borracho nos tiró un costal de harina de 24 libras. Más tarde nos dijeron que además de borracho también iba grifo. Me asusté, sí, pero no tanto como cuando me topé con el hijo de un vecino que estaba loco. Yo llevaba una pinta de leche en botella de vidrio y cuando se me apareció el pobre loco, solté la botella y me puse a correr tan recio que me pasé de mi casa. Por cierto tiempo yo hacía cualquier cosa en casa menos ir por el mandado.

En un restorán de Ruffing no dejaban entrar a la raza, en otro sí. Puede ser que en el primero lo dejarían entrar a uno pero no le servirían, lo que viene siendo casi lo mismo. En el segundo estábamos papá y yo cuando vimos a una familia negra, el señor, la señora y dos hijitos de la edad mía, sobre poco más o menos. Papá dijo que a los negritos nomás les servían en la cocina y que, en otros restoranes, ni en la cocina. No le entendí a papá muy bien aunque me lo dijo dos o tres veces. ¿Cómo haría el negro para que sus hijos le entendieran?

En Monon, Indiana, en la ruta 421, hay un café que se llama Myrtle's que está a dos cuadras de una gasolinera Shell. En la Shell nos parábamos a echarle gas al troque cuando íbamos a Benton Harbor; a la cherry. Cuando parábamos allí yo iba con papá a comprar donas en que Myrtle's. Una vez la señora le dijo a papá que yo ya me estaba haciendo grandecito. En el troque papá me dijo que ya eran seis veces que yo hacía el viaje a Michigan.

Un año escaso después que se había muerto mi papá, recibimos una esquela que anunciaba la muerte de una señora en Ruffing. Yo tendría unos trece años y no sabía quién podría ser. Mamá no fue al entierro pero nos exigió a que fuéramos mis hermanos y yo, para cumplir, como decía ella. Rumbo a Ruffing, Ismael me explicó que esa señora muerta era media hermana nuestra; una hija que tuvo papá de otra mujer. Conociendo a mamá como la conocía y a papá como lo conocí, me di cuenta que vivía entre extraños. Cuando llegamos, la gente nos saludó de mano, dimos los pésames y nos dieron sillas en la primera fila del velorio.

Pónganle un pedazo de hielo en la frente y así se le para la sangre. Bueno; ahora, la cabeza atrás, así; pero con cuidado de que no se vaya a ahogar. ¿Y tú? ¿Qué estás haciendo allí, paradote, nomás? ¿No ves cómo está tu hermanito? Bien le decía yo a tu papá que no te dieran la licencia de manejar; que estabas muy chico. Ándale, vete a casa y allí me esperas.

A ver, señoritas, hagan sala —aquí vienen unos señores norteamericanos.

Qué señores, ni qué americanos, ni qué nada; éramos Monche Rivera y yo. A la puta que a mí me tocó se le translucía el vestido; yo tenía quince años y un miedo de la chingada.

Cuando en Corea, todo lo que comíamos era de polvo. Cayo Díaz decía que el Army nos daba papas con huevo para el desayuno, huevos con papas para la comida y papas a huevo para la cena.

En un Rest y Recuperation en Japón, con Cayo Díaz y Balderas, otro buddy del Triple Nickel (555 Field Artillery Bn., Major Oscar Warren, Commanding) después de una parranda que empezamos en Tokyo, amanecimos en un tren que iba a Kobe. En el primer sentón, Cayo se echó catorce Asahi *birus,* después: baño, vieja y verija. Cómo andaría yo que para el tercer día me puse a cantar aquello de "llegando al puente me devolví . . . "

Muchas familias de Klail, de Flora y de Bascom se conocen bien; otras, además, están emparentadas. A pesar de todo eso, cuando uno de Klail, pongamos por caso, se va a casar con una de Flora, siempre mandan una comitiva a que vaya a pedir a la novia. Entonces los hombres se ponen corbatas y se ponen muy serios. Los novios se ponen nerviosos; él suda y ella se abanica.

En Relámpago tengo un pariente que le dicen La Caballona. Flojo y huevón, vive de lo que le dan en casa. Cuando le avisaron que Paula, su novia, se había echado con todos los que vivíamos en Relámpago, La Caballona respondió: "¿Y qué? ¿Qué tan grande es Relámpago?"

Cuando el menor de los Murillo le dijo a don Víctor Solís que quería calar a Estefanita antes de casarse con ella, don Víctor le dijo que su hija no era ninguna sandía. El menor de los Murillo se creía muy águila y todos, menos él, sabían cada vez que su mujer le ponía tamaños cuernos.

Cuando Pancho "La Burra" se largó con el dinero en el pot del World Series, la gente decía que así que volviera a Bascom le iban a dar una santa paliza. A fin de tres meses volvió Pancho, montado en una bicicleta azul listo para vender números de la rifa. Como dijo el Argentino: En realidad, uno no sabe qué pensar de la gente.

En Bascom unos siempre andaban con el susidio de no relajar a la raza: Pórtate bien; ¿qué dirán los bolillos? Lo triste del caso es que a los bolillos les importaba madre lo que uno hiciera. Oh, it's nothing, you know. Just one of them Mexicans having a fight in a cantina . . . They play one of them rancheras on the jukebox and then one lets out a squeal . . . first thing you know they's having theirselves a fight.

¡Qué bonito, chingao!

Cuando el del banco se dio un tiro todo mundo supo por qué. La familia, con su buen seguro, vivió bien y se acabó. Cuando Chale Villalón se robó una jersey y un football todo mundo se dio cuenta; el heroico Board of Education ordenó al condestable que lo arrestara para que aprendiera que con la escuela no se jugaba.

Rafa, así que entre Echevarría, no le vendas cerveza.

¿Anda pedo o qué?

Pedo y terco, ya lo conoces.

¿Y qué le digo?

A ver si tratas de ver que ya no tome.

Entra Echevarría, pedo.

Quiero una Buddy Watson.

No hay Budweiser.

¿Y Hamm's, no hay Hamm's?

Se acabaron.

¿Hay Lonestor?

No hay Lone Star.

¿Tienen Yax?

Tampoco.

¿Y qué tal Flagstaff . . . hay Flag?

Menos.

¿Qué hay, entonces?

Pura Perla.

¿Perla? ¡Venga la Perla!

Pero nomás en quarts.

Mejor, así no se me acaban tan pronto.

Están al tiempo.

¡Qué suerte! Así no me pongo ronco.

Un señor que se cansa:

¡Con una chingada! ¡Véndanle a Echevarría lo que quiera!

El día que Tome Fonseca le pegó a Robe Cantú en el billar de Pérez con la bola colorada (la número tres) la palomilla le cambió de sobrenombre. Es más, el apodo estaba en inglés y en menos de un mes ya respondía a Three. A Cantú, en verdad, le hicieron un favor porque es sumamente difícil lucirse cuando a uno le llaman "Cagón".

¡A veinte!
¡La tuya!
¡Zafo!
¡Una más arriba de todas las que hables!
¡Me la pelas!
¡Siéntate!
¡Me sacas la blanca!

Se hizo demasiado largo el palabreo y, a decir verdad, ninguno quería pelear. De suerte que alguien no les dijo que mejor se fueran a dormir juntos porque entonces sí se comprometían y tendrían que darse en la madre. Otros, con menos suerte, se han muerto a consecuencia de lo que diga un mirón.

Enterramos a mamá. Es la tercera vez que he llorado. En mi vida.

El que antes se encargó del Draft Board ahora la hace de Veterans' Adviser. La raza pendeja decía que sus patrones lo apreciaban mucho y que por eso tenía buen jale. Shit.

Me voy a Austin; a la universidad. A ver qué sale. No voy a desperdiciar el G.I. Bill como mi hermano Ismael que se casó y se jodió.

Pueblo nuevo, vida nueva. Veremos.

Also by / También por Rolando Hinojosa

A Voice of My Own: Essays and Stories

Ask a Policeman: A Rafe Buenrostro Mystery

Becky and Her Friends

Dear Rafe / Mi querido Rafa

Klail City

Los amigos de Becky

Partners in Crime: A Rafe Buenrostro Mystery

Rites and Witnesses

The Useless Servants

We Happy Few